Being under the k

He wasn't suppose— him. He has nothing to lose, no one he trusts, and revenge on his mind.

Not exactly the insta-boyfriend you were promised he would be.

Ashley took the knife home as a joke, but there's nothing funny about her attraction to an angry and possibly homicidal utensil.

Maybe some knives deserve to be left in the drawer.

His lack of memory of the events that led to his unit being trapped in silverware isn't cutting it.

Ray is the reason your mother always told you to be careful with knives. Play with him and he might hurt you without even meaning to.

But when danger starts circling, and you need protection, it's wiser to reach for a knife than a spoon.

Cautionary warning:
The humor in this novella is sharp. Not for the thin-skinned. Please be aware that all of the scenes are fictional and should not be tried at home. Not even my editor would act them out to check for feasibility. Extreme care should be employed when considering viewing a knife as a potential mate.

KNIFED
A Lighthearted Utensil Romance
Book 3

Ruth Cardello

Author Contact
website: RuthCardello.com
email: rcardello@ruthcardello.com
Facebook: Author Ruth Cardello
TikTok: tiktok.com/@author.ruthcardello

Copyright

Knifed: A Lighthearted Utensil Romance
Copyright © 2024 by Ruth Cardello
Print Edition

ISBN eBook: 978-1-963122-27-5
ISBN Print: 978-1-963122-28-2

An Original work by Ruth Cardello

All Rights Reserved

This book or any portion thereof may not be reproduced or used in any manner whatsoever without the express written permission of the copyright owner except for the use of brief quotations in a book review.

This is a work of fiction. Any resemblance to actual persons, places, events, business establishments or locales is entirely coincidental

This book is dedicated to:

This book is dedicated to quirky, kind-hearted heroes. The world is a better place because you're in it.

Trigger warning:
This novella is about a World War II super soldier with a history of abuse that left him damaged both physically and mentally. Due to his sharp nature, the author chose to not portray certain intimate scenes in detail. If it sounded painful in my imagination, it didn't make it on paper. Also, oddly enough, it's challenging to come up with quality knife jokes. I apologize in advance for my attempts.

Note to my readers

I didn't expect to enjoy writing in this cutlery world as much as I have. I was certain the entire story could be told in three books... and then Ashley's mother wanted a super soldier *or three* of her own. I will return to writing billionaire romances, but I may have to write one last utensil romance... a *why choose* for Ashley's mom. Doesn't every mom deserve a little fun now and then?

Chapter One

Ray

I CAN'T BREATHE.

I'm drowning, but in what?

How can I be here yet not here at the same time?

I feel someone pulling me toward the surface, but relief doesn't come. I'm alone again, disorientated, and trapped.

I try to make sense of my situation, but rather than thinking clearly, I'm bombarded by images from when I was much younger. I'm not in control, and I can't escape. I know this feeling and this place, but this time, there are no walls to kick against and no wood to scrape my nails into.

I'm not in the trunk my father tossed me into so no one would see my bloodied body or hear my screams. I swing with fury but connect with nothing. Am I in the hospital? Or still on the path waiting to be found?

I don't want to be here. I don't want to wake up more helpless than I was before my father took me deep into the woods and left me to die. Broken. Unable to move either of my legs.

God, what if they give me back to him? If I'm still on the path, let me die here. I'm not the reason my mother left him—the way he treated both of us was. Never kind. Rarely sober. I shouldn't have told him it was his fault she ran off. I should have run, too, but I was angry with both of them. Why didn't she take me with her? Maybe I'm the problem.

No.

I don't think of myself that way anymore.

I will never be that person again.

I remember hauling my battered body far enough out of the woods to be found. I refused to rest—refused to die. He didn't win. I did.

I try to move a finger then an eyelid. Nothing happens, just as the swing I took was only in my thoughts.

There was a hospital. Bright lights. Soothing voices. Was I rescued or is this what my brain is offering up to comfort me in my last moments?

More memories fill my thoughts, and I need them to be real. I need to have survived to leave the hospital in a wheelchair and be taken in by my aunt. She told me she'd found a way I could be useful and handed me over to strangers who promised they could heal me. Project Inkwell. I need to have joined them, survived the injections, and gone off to Europe to save the world.

I was the problem. Weak. Easily broken. Unlovable. Not now. That me died with each of Inkwell's injections. Even those in my unit are careful to stay on my good side.

My unit.

They're real.

I've freed the innocent.

Hunted down those who would bring more evil into the world.

I'm a hero—a strong man, unstoppable and ruthless.

With a primal cry, I call upon the rage of someone who has been held down and hurt. It rises in me, replacing every bit of my humanity with whatever it was that gave me the strength to pull my half-paralyzed body along the ground without stopping to rest.

The power of rage is as real and raw as it is ugly. I unleash it on whatever it is that is imprisoning me.

I reject this place.

I reject this weakness.

I demand to be released.

Now.

Chapter Two

Ashley

"GREG!" I CALL out and rise to my feet as he enters the sandwich shop. It could be jitters from the second coffee I downed in the last hour, but my hands are cold and shaky.

Several women look him over as he makes his way to me. Greg is tall, toned, and well-dressed, with a mop of hair that always looks slightly mussed. More than once, I've suggested him as dating potential to our mutual friend Cheryl. She's not interested.

I'm not either.

Why? I don't know. There's nothing *wrong* with him, but he doesn't set my heart racing either. He's easy-going and I could imagine living with him, but I could also imagine living without him and I want more than that.

He slides into the chair across from me and I retake my seat. "Sorry I didn't answer your text earlier, I was sleeping in. Everything okay?"

I drum my fingers on the table. "I think so. I hope so. Cheryl said she was on her way then never showed up. Thanks for coming. I was going crazy sitting here alone."

"Did you try calling her?"

"She's not answering."

"Her phone might have died."

"Maybe."

"You look upset." He nods as if something just occurred to him. "Is this about Leo? If so, you did break his heart a little, but he says he's okay to still hang out."

I look away then back to meet his gaze. Leo and I are good. At least, I think so. I told him I want to go back to being friends. He seemed to take the news well. "It's Cheryl. She's been ghosting me. That's not like her. I don't know if she had a thing for him and hates me now or if there's something going on with her that she's afraid to tell me. Has she been acting strange with you?"

He chokes on a sarcastic laugh. "Oh, yeah."

"Every time I try to make plans with her lately, she says she's too busy." It's strange to pour my heart out to Greg. He and I don't have that kind of friendship, but here we are.

"At least she's taking your call, she sends me to voicemail."

"Ouch." I drum my fingers on the table. "That's not like her. Something must be going on. She did say she was considering switching jobs. Maybe she decided to. That can be overwhelming."

"Maybe."

Greg looks guilty. He's not good at hiding his emotions. "What did you do?"

He steeples his fingers. "Nothing."

I wait.

He lowers his hands. "I *may* have suggested that we could fuck."

"You and Cheryl?" He didn't think . . . no, he couldn't mean me.

"Yes, Cheryl."

"Okay." Still, I hadn't seen that one coming. I mean, I probably should have, since Cheryl had recently told me she was considering diddling a spoon. She was lonely. "Well, now everything makes sense. So, are you two together?"

"No."

"I get it. She doesn't want to face me because we can't keep secrets from each other and shit like this is embarrassing. No wonder she doesn't want to hear about Leo. She made the same mistake with you."

"We didn't have sex."

"She turned you down?"

"She did."

"Wow. I guess she's not as lonely as I thought."

"Ouch. Man with feelings over here."

"Sorry." I search his face. "You okay?"

"Yeah. It is what it is."

I sigh. "If it makes you feel better, today I made one joke

and she became completely unhinged. She's obviously stressed about something."

A smile returns to his face. "It can't be us."

I smile back. "Are *we* the drama? No."

"So, what was the joke that sent her over the edge?"

I weigh the harm in telling him. We both love Cheryl. And Mercedes was Greg's friend before she was mine. Plus, I can't be the only one who finds the situation hilarious. "Okay, so Mercedes told Cheryl something that Cheryl wasn't supposed to tell anyone."

Greg leans closer. "What?"

"I'm not supposed to say."

His eyebrows come together slightly. "You put it in the vault."

"I did."

"You can tell me."

"I cannot."

"What if I guess?"

See, Greg is fun. Life doesn't have to be so serious all the time. "I can't say a word."

"Slow blink once for yes. Fast blink three times for no."

I chuckle. "Fine."

"Is it about Hugh?"

I slow blink once.

He continues, "Is the engagement off?"

I quickly blink three times.

"Is she pregnant?"

Three more fast blinks.

"Did they have a fight?"

More fast blinking.

"Does he have a criminal past?"

My eyelids begin to tire as I blink quickly three times again.

"Does he have a disease?"

I sigh. "You're not even close."

He throws up his hands in frustration. "So, give me a clue."

I hold up a fork.

He frowns. "He's a picky eater?"

I slam the fork down. "Why would that be a secret?"

He shrugs. "He's a dork? Stork? Mork?"

"What are you doing?"

"Does the secret rhyme with fork?"

"This isn't charades." I give up on blinking.

"Does what Mercedes told her start with an F?"

"No."

"The fork is made of stainless steel. Steal. Is he a thief?"

"I already said he's not a criminal."

"I need another hint."

I close my eyes and pinch the bridge of my nose. "You've met Hugh and you're Mercedes' friend. Do they not talk to you about their relationship?"

He puts up three fingers "They want to be a throuple?"

"No."

"She's upset that he doesn't have a job? And now they can't eat?"

"No."

"Mercedes still has feelings for me?"

"Wait? What? You and she . . .?"

"No, but she asked me out once. Right before Hugh came back."

I did not know that. "This isn't about you."

"Is it about you?"

"No."

He scratches his chin. "Give me another clue."

With my hands flat on the table, my patience snaps. "Mercedes and Hugh have this inside joke about being inappropriately attracted to silverware."

"I'm sorry—what?"

"She thinks he's a fork."

"Hugh?"

"Yeah. It's a fun little fantasy she and Hugh have. She pretends he's a fork and they fuck."

"That's the strangest fantasy I've ever heard."

"You don't even know the half of it."

He cocks his head to one side. "Tell me."

I hesitate because he looks interested in the topic, but not amused by it. "Hugh's the reason Mercedes asked us to research Project Inkwell."

"Really?"

"Yeah, he must have heard about Project Inkwell somewhere and loved the idea of it. He pretends to be . . . or he believes he is . . . a super soldier from WWII."

"Odd."

"Right?"

"He looks young for someone who'd be about a hundred years old."

"His explanation is that he and his unit have spent the last eighty years trapped in silverware."

"*Which* silverware? The box she keeps in her kitchen?"

His tone gives me goosebumps. Since when is he serious? A sudden urge to lie to him has me saying, "I don't know. It's all a fantasy, anyway."

Cheryl bursts into the restaurant, followed by a tall, bear of a man. Hugh and Mercedes are on their heels.

They surround us. Both Greg and I stand up.

"Hi, Greg," Mercedes says quickly.

"Hi, Mercedes," he responds.

Looking frazzled, Cheryl glances at the man at her side then at Greg. "Greg, we'll explain later, but right now we need to talk to Ashley. Alone."

"All of you?" he looks from one to the next of them. "Whatever's going on, you know I won't judge. I'll help."

Cheryl shakes her head vehemently. "Not this time. Not yet. I don't want to hurt your feelings, Greg, but this isn't something that involves you. So . . ."

Greg straightens and flexes his shoulders back. "I thought we were friends."

"We are," Mercedes says in a rush, before meeting Cheryl's gaze. "We could just tell him. You guys have been Greg's friend longer than I have. Can't we trust him?"

Cheryl turns to me and the fear in her eyes is the only reason I hold my silence. Greg's feelings come second to whatever has Cheryl in a panic and I don't like the expression on his face. He doesn't look hurt . . . he looks like he's pretending to be hurt.

Greg holds out his hand to the man at Cheryl's side. "I'll go, but since I feel like we'll meet again—Hello, I'm Greg."

The large man shakes Greg's hand. "Jack."

After dropping Jack's hand, Greg nods at Mercedes' fiancé. "Hugh."

"Greg," he responds.

After one last look around at us, Greg says, "Call me if you need me."

"We will," Cheryl assures him.

"Don't look so sad," Mercedes says in the sympathetic tone one might use with a child. "We'll all get together soon."

"Whatever," Greg growls before turning on his heel and walking out.

I would normally have gone after him to make sure he's okay, but my attention is glued to the man who is now holding Cheryl's hand. "Jack? Jack as in *Spoon* Jack?"

Cheryl steps closer. "Lower your voice and yes. *Spoon* Jack."

My mouth rounds then I let out a bark of a laugh. "This is a joke, right?"

"We shouldn't talk here," Hugh says firmly. "How far is your apartment?"

"Just a block or so." Now that I've had time to get a good look at them, they all seem a little shell-shocked. "Seriously, what's going on?"

Cheryl and Jack exchange a look then she says, "We'll explain everything—at your apartment."

"Fine," I say and grab the trash off my table and deposit it in a bin.

Mercedes falls into step beside me as soon as we're on the sidewalk. "This is all my fault. I shouldn't have involved you—especially not while we're still figuring out what to do next. When you ran your hand over the silverware... I wasn't thinking about who might be in each piece or that there might be an order for the unit to come back. I just wanted to help."

"What are you talking about?"

Cheryl flanks my other side. "Mercedes, wait until we're somewhere we can all talk. And this isn't your fault. It's mine. If I had told Ashley everything, she wouldn't have chosen the knife."

Chapter Three

Ray

PAPERS FLY IN all directions as I spread out across a shiny white surface. It's cold and hard against my forehead. I push myself off it with enough force that I land on my feet a yard from what I realize is a desk.

Where the hell am I?

A quick glance down confirms I'm in my dress uniform but my chest is covered with medals I don't remember receiving. My head is pounding, my muscles are spasming, and the room blurs out of focus. I stumble backward into a bookcase and catch myself before I hit the floor.

Why am I weak?

What's wrong with my legs?

A wave of nausea washes over me and I close my eyes briefly, determined to not throw up all over myself before I at least know where I am. Wherever I am, escape may require blending in, and that will be difficult if I soil the front of my jacket.

Feeling slightly steadier on my feet, I straighten and look around. I'm in what appears to be a feminine office. The decor is sage green and white. There's a tan couch with a white plush throw across it. The shiny surface I flung myself from is the top of a futuristic-looking desk. All around my feet sketches of odd-looking toys are scattered. Machines in clothing? I can't tell and honestly, I don't care enough to put much thought into them.

I have no idea where I am or how I got here. As soon as I'm free of this place, I'll find my unit and figure out what happened to me. I head toward the open door of the office but freeze when I hear a voice.

"Jack, this is the only way."

Recognizing that voice brings a sense of relief. Hugh's not my favorite person, but I might hug him anyway. If I live long enough to. The persistent pain in my head is confusing. I heal so fast now that I haven't experienced discomfort at this level for a long time.

When I first joined Inkwell the injections we received killed many men. If you lived, you gained enhanced physical abilities and were able to regenerate body parts. However, there was no predicting or stopping the death of someone once they began to reject the treatments. It was something we knew could happen at any time. It's been years since we've lost a man that way and even longer since any of us have received a dose.

Our handlers at Inkwell expected our transformation to

cease when the injections did, but the speed at which we heal is still increasing. Broken bones now mend in moments rather than months.

Whatever is wrong with me should be fleeting, but the pain is getting worse rather than lessening. This is not how I'd hoped to die. After everything we've done, it feels anticlimactic and disappointing.

Do I want Hugh to see me this way? I begin walking toward the door. If there is any part of my death that can help him or the others, he needs to know what's happening to me. I hear Hugh say, "Ray's too dangerous. He can't come back now."

Can't come back? From where? I shudder as my memory produces a painfully vivid image of the place I just escaped.

"He's already awakening," Jack says.

Jack.

Of all the men in my unit, Jack's the one I'd say I trust the most, but something in his tone has me tensing. Why don't they want me awake?

Did they drug me? I strain to remember anything before landing on the desk a few minutes ago. There was the weird dream about a woman and before that . . . before that . . .

Memories flood in of men being taken in the middle of the night by armed guards from Project Inkwell. The honor of working for Inkwell came at a steep price. Second chances weren't given. If a man stepped out of line, he was removed and dealt with. No warning. No reason given.

We haven't lost a man since we swore to stand together, even against our government. There wasn't a change in policy, but I figured we'd become strong enough that attempting to take one of us would have proven difficult, if it were even still possible.

How had Inkwell convinced Jack and Hugh to turn on me?

What did I do? There's a dark shadow looming in my memories, blocking me from remembering, but whispering this is my fault.

What's my fault?

What can't I remember?

"Where's the knife, Ashley?" Hugh demands. "Let's do this quickly and get it over with."

Fuck, Hugh is planning to slice me to pieces. It's the most sensible method. A bullet is rarely instantly deadly. I could regenerate as fast as he could shoot. But if he severs my head? Dead is dead and dead can't heal.

He must think I'm unconscious and vulnerable. The searing pain in my head nearly has me in that condition. What the hell did they drug me with? Why can't my body fight it?

"In my office on the desk," a female voice says softly. I recognize the voice and it calls to me, but my adrenaline is pumping, and I need to stay focused. I've survived worse. I'll survive this.

I move to one side to listen better without being seen. A

quick glance at the desk puts me slightly more at ease when there's no knife on it. I may be unarmed, but I have the element of surprise and I intend to use it.

"I can't do this to Ray," Jack says in a tone that doesn't convince me he'll do much to protect me. "We're brothers first. We stand and fight as one or fall and die together. Remember?" My stomach churns. A part of me always knew Jack was all talk. The most dangerous enemies a person can have are the ones who pretend to be friends. Hugh never liked me, so learning he's not loyal to me isn't a surprise, but Jack's betrayal guts me.

"Don't *brothers first* me. You also have doubts about him. We need to act now before it's too late."

"It's already too late."

"Stand down, Jack." The voices grow louder as they approach.

Jack snaps, "*You* stand down. You're not in charge anymore, Hugh."

I grimace. Jack almost sounds like he has a spine.

Hugh says, "You think I want to do this? We don't have a choice."

"There's always a choice."

The discord evident in their chatter is a good sign. If they're at odds with each other, they'll be easier to beat. Hugh and Jack, when they work in unison, are a force none of us have won against. But one at a time? I could take them out.

I've done it before.

I'll do it this time.

Jack's back fills the doorway. "There's a lot we don't understand about our situation, but Ray saved my ass more than once. I won't do this."

I take a deep breath. Okay, so maybe Jack is on my side. Maybe this fight will be us against Hugh.

Hugh's tone is as dry and pompous as always. "Your ass wouldn't have needed saving if he could stick to a plan."

When Jack doesn't immediately answer, I tense. Yes, some of my ideas have nearly gotten Jack and me killed but that's only because I don't play it safe like Hugh does. The parameters of our missions have never been as clear-cut to me as they are to him.

We're tasked with saving the world, but are we supposed to stand back and ignore atrocities simply because they have nothing to do with our orders? Why have superhuman strength if not to use it to protect those who cannot protect themselves?

Hugh and his fucking ego. He likes to take credit for our wins, but I'm the one who goes in first, takes the hits, and gets results. So, yeah, sometimes that means Jack needs to carry my battered body out, but I'm the reason we never retreat—never fail. It's my courage that's the torch the men follow through the darkness. Without me, we would have never discovered how near death we could be and still heal.

I stand motionless and silent. It's not pain or my mortality that I fear, but I'll be damned if Hugh is what ends me. If Director Falcon has decided to remove me, he'll need to come kill me himself.

"Ray will—" Jack begins, but Hugh cuts him off.

"Endanger all of us? He's impulsive and reckless. You know he'll expose us. Are you willing to risk the lives of everyone else for him? Risk everything you have here—even Cheryl?"

Cheryl? Who the fuck is she?

"I hate that you might be right." And just like that, Jack's loyalty dissolves like sand beneath an ocean wave.

Fuck him.

Fuck both of them.

This is not when and where I'll die.

I can't say the same for them.

In a move I've honed to perfection, I rush up behind Jack, take his head between my hands, and give it a neck-breaking twist. Unprepared, he doesn't have the time to tense and drops to the floor. Maybe dead. Maybe not. I'll know in a few minutes because we heal fast.

I step on Jack's back, reach forward, and haul Hugh over him. The room spins, but I fight to stay focused. I have the element of surprise and I don't waste it. Hugh will aim for my arms and legs first. That's his go-to strategy. So, as I lift him, I crush both of his upper arms in my hands then swing him upward with such force that I hear the bones in his legs crack.

All the sparring we've done in preparation of fighting others has revealed an unfortunate weakness in all of us . . . although we are stronger and faster, we are just as breakable.

I have the upper hand, and I'm taking full advantage of it. There's screaming—from more than one woman. I don't stop. I can't show mercy. Given the chance, Hugh will kill me.

Not today, my friend, not today.

I swing Hugh back and forth against the doorframe, until his skull cracks and he's limp in my arms. In a sparring match, this is where I would stop. Nothing I've done to him won't heal if there's even a fraction of life left in him.

The mountain beneath me shifts. I stumble and drop Hugh's now motionless body. "That's enough, Ray," Jack growls.

Two enormous arms encircle me from behind and lift me off my feet. Three women surround Hugh. One is crying. A second is frantically reassuring the first that he'll heal. A third woman moves to stand in front of Hugh and meets my gaze.

Time stills, and for just a second, it feels as if she and I have stepped outside of that brutal scene. There's fear in her eyes, but also compassion. I've never seen her before, but I recognize her as the woman in my dream. I open my mouth to ask her who she is, but Jack steps back from Hugh and turns away from her carrying me with him.

My hands close around his forearms. He tosses me forward before I can do any damage. I hit the wall head-first and slide down. As soon as my feet touch the floor, I spin.

Jack is there, standing with his feet apart, like a human shield protecting Hugh. "Calm down, Ray."

"And make killing me easy? No thanks." I lean forward and quickly assess my options for attack. He matches my stance.

"No one wants to kill you. We're here to help you."

I circle slowly to the left then to the right. Jack is fast on his feet, but I'm faster. All I need is an opening. "Unfortunately for you, I'm not deaf. You had me fooled for a while there, Jack. All that talk of watching out for each other. I never really believed it, though. I knew this day would come."

"You're confused, Ray. I was too. This whole situation is fucked up."

"No, what's fucked up is you staying to fight me instead of running while you can. I've always liked you, Jack. Leave now and you'll be dead to me, but still alive enough to have to live with yourself and the knowledge that you're a piece of shit."

Jack raises both hands in a request for a truce. "I'm not going anywhere because I'm on your side, Ray. Always have been."

"Then I'm sorry this is the way you'll die." I reach beside me, grab a lamp, snap the top off, and throw it like a dagger at him. He moves to the side and it pierces the wall. When he glances back at it, I lunge.

Jack is taller than I am and built like a rhino, but I have a skill he's never mastered—the art of zero hesitation. I sweep his legs out from beneath him and as he goes down, I hammer my hand into his face with a series of powerful punches.

He rolls away, shaking his head, blood pouring from his nose and lip. "Calm the fuck down, Ray. You have no idea where you are or what's going on. Stop and listen before I'm forced to hurt you."

"Before *you* hurt *me?*" My vision blurs again and my thoughts jumble. He's not Jack anymore, he's my father, yelling that everything he did to me was my fault. I let out a primal snarl and grab Jack off the floor by his neck and hold him above me. His hands grip my fingers to pry them off, but my rage amplifies my strength to beyond even his.

His eyes bulge, and his confidence wavers as the realization kicks in that I'm not letting go, and he won't survive this. I could end him quickly, but I need to know why. Why me? Why now?

He's struggling to breathe and my hold on him lessens slightly as another wave of pain rocks through me. I stumble backward, still holding him above me.

"Stop," a woman says urgently before she sprays a white substance all over my face. I wipe it out of my eyes with my free hand. Some of it gets into my mouth. Is that sweet cream? In a tone a mother might use with a wayward child, she says, "You're getting blood all over my rug and my landlord is a real dick about not refunding security deposits."

Jack lands a rib-shattering punch to my chest. I drop him and double over. He sends me face down to the floor with a hit to the back of my neck. I groan and roll over just in time for the kick that sends me flying across the room and over the desk. The wall crumbles beneath the impact and I bounce with momentum to the floor.

After a breath, I roll and lift the desk over my head with the intention of throwing it at Jack, when a liquid splashes me in the face, temporarily blinding me. I shake the water off and look down. Right in front of me, a woman who's at least a foot and a half shorter than I am is waving an empty glass at me. Her skirt is short, her blouse tight and open enough to reveal a distracting amount of rounded breast. I can't look away. She's a little bit warrior and a whole lot of siren. Fearlessly, she commands, "Put that desk down right now. I saved up for a year to buy that."

"Who the fuck are you?"

Her chin rises and she holds my gaze boldly. "I'm the woman who rents this apartment. And it was not easy to get a place in this neighborhood. I sat on a waiting list for months. So, unless you and your friends want to move this super-soldier pissing contest outside, you need to stop."

I let out a half-laugh half-cough. "Sorry, just fighting for my life over here."

Jack's quick approach steals my attention from her. I

lower the desk to the floor. He's now too close for it to be worth the toss. I motion for him to bring his best.

Without looking away from me, Jack says, "It's not safe in here, Ashley. Take Cheryl and Mercedes outside." He grabs a floor lamp and smashes the end of it until the base breaks off, then holds it in front of him like it's some fucking weapon.

"That's my other favorite lamp," she mutters, then says, "Mercedes, do something."

"I wish I could." The woman on her knees beside Hugh answers in a thick voice. "Hugh is healing, but he's still unconscious."

"Cheryl?" Ashley asks.

"I don't know what you think I can do." The third woman passes her question along, "Jack?"

Jack flexes his hands on the pole he's holding. "Ray, all I want to do is talk to you. If you give me a chance to explain what's going on, no one gets hurt."

Pain cuts through my skull again. I bend over and gasp for air. "What did you do to me?" I snarl. "Did you poison me or something?"

"We didn't do anything to you. Ray, we're all in the same boat. Something happened to us at the award dinner. It's how we all ended up here—"

"I don't remember the award dinner."

Jack and I begin to circle each other. "What do you remember?" he asks.

"Director Falcon wanted to see me. We had a drink—" Something smashes into the back of my head and I drop to my knees.

Hugh is up and back in the mix. Weaker than before because he's still healing and that's a mistake. At full strength, with the support of Jack, he could have beaten me. But the knee he brings to my chin barely snaps my head back.

All talking ends.

I pummel Hugh. Jack comes in from the side and attempts to remove me. When that fails, he starts trying to take me down. He has a punch that can easily send a man into next week, but I've learned to move fast enough to lessen the power of them.

Snap. Crackle. Pop. The three of us are on the ground, tearing each other apart, breaking whatever we can reach. It's a fucking bloody mess, but I'm holding my own.

"Ray!" the woman named Ashley calls out my name.

I look up and freeze when she whips open her shirt, revealing gorgeous tits with only the nipples covered with circles of white lace. I could bury my face in her cleavage, but her breasts are also perky enough for me to understand why they don't submit to the indignity of confinement.

She stands there, hands on hips, breasts bouncing like some female goddess and I don't know what to do with how possessive I feel toward a woman I don't know.

Jack stills and looks up at Ashley as well. The reason for wanting him dead a moment ago is replaced by a fresh desire to punch him in the face for not averting his eyes.

That's my woman.

Mine.

Wait? What?

"Whoever just got a boner needs to get the hell off my leg," Hugh growls as he disengages his limbs from mine.

"That wasn't me," Jack announces and jumps to his feet looking across the room toward one of the women. "Because I didn't even look at her."

The woman responds, "Ashley, put your damn shirt back on before I send Jack back to Mercedes and trade him out for a spoon who doesn't ogle my friends."

"Cheryl, I couldn't *not* look," Jack asserts. "I've only ever seen one woman."

Like a skit in a comedy, Jack and Cheryl step away to talk about something that is apparently more important than killing me. I scan the room for Hugh, who is talking softly to the woman I believe is named Mercedes.

What the hell is going on here?

I slowly rise to my feet and meet Ashley's gaze. The embarrassment I expected to see in her eyes isn't there. She closes her shirt and slowly rebuttons it. I'm mesmerized, and with my cock bulging in my pants, I can't deny that she has a potent effect on me.

Her hands settle back on her hips. "Do I have your attention now?"

"You do." I swallow hard and gulp a breath. She's beautiful. Spirited. Brave.

But there's another layer to this—I feel connected to her.

Shaking my head, I try to dislodge the distraction of my attraction to her. Women are off-limits to everyone in my unit and have been for years. How does this one know Jack and Hugh? And why is everyone dressed so oddly?

Pain. Fuck. And not from the broken skin and bones that are healing. I double over again, gripping my hands on my knees, and inhale slowly several times.

"Are you okay?" Ashley asks as she steps closer. Her hand goes to my forehead. "You're burning up." To the others, she says, "He has a fever. I thought you guys couldn't get sick."

In an instant, both Hugh and Jack are at my side. A hand that was only a moment ago doing its best to break me, now rests on my forehead briefly. "She's right," Jack announces. "What are you on, Ray? We agreed not to take those drugs anymore."

I shake my head and my vision blurs. "I didn't take anything."

The woman beside Jack says, "He said he had a drink with Director Falcon. Someone might have put something in it."

Hugh nods. "That's possible." He turns to Ashley. "Was he like this when you . . . you know . . . brought him back?"

Ashley shakes her head. "I didn't bring him back."

Mercedes touches her arm. "Don't be embarrassed, we've all done it . . . even if it is just eating from him."

"I didn't eat with the knife and I certainly didn't fuck it. So, I don't know how this happened, but it wasn't me." Ashley waves her hands in my direction.

"Could there have been another woman here?" Mercedes asks.

Ashley looks around at the bloodied and tattered room and shrugs. "I don't see how there could have been, but if there was, she's welcome to him."

Jack uses the back of his hand to wipe blood from his cheek. "Was there someone with you when you came back, Ray? If so, we need to find her. You'll need her if you accidentally go back."

"Go back where? What are you talking about?" None of this makes any sense.

Jack sighs. "I don't know how much to tell you before we find her. I struggled with the truth when I first heard it."

"I did as well," Hugh says quietly.

"Will someone, anyone, fucking explain what's going on?" I growl.

Ashley folds her arms beneath those gorgeous but now sadly covered breasts of hers. "Something happened to your unit at the award dinner. You've been locked inside a knife for eighty years. And before you ask: Yes, we won the war. No, you didn't actually save anyone. And, yes, we won by creating the very weapon your mission was to save the world from. Also, apparently, I chose the only piece of silverware that doesn't require sex to transform back. So, even in the world of cutlery, I'm unlucky in love."

"Is any of this really happening?" I double over again and this time sink to my knees. A wave of nausea washes over me, but I don't let it win.

"We should get him to a bed," Jack says.

Ashley wedges herself beneath one of my arms as if she'll be able to carry my weight. I straighten but allow myself the pleasure of keeping her tucked to my side. "By all means, let's slide that bloody body of his beneath my pure white duvet because my dream bedroom might as well match my dream office."

Mercedes takes my other arm. "We'll clean it up. All of us. We're in this together. Right, Hugh?"

I glance back at Hugh. He's watching me closely, his expression difficult to decipher. "Is this hell?" I ask.

"No," he says quietly. "It's somewhere much better and much worse."

Too exhausted to try to make sense of that, I allow Ashley and Mercedes to lead me down a hallway to her bedroom. I'm sore from my injuries in a way I'm not used to. One of my fingers is still broken. Is it possible that I'm losing my ability to heal?

Ashley moves to stand in front of me and, without asking permission, begins to undo my tie. "Let's get him out of these clothes and wash off the blood before we put him in my bed. Mercedes, are you okay with this or do you want me to ask Cheryl to help me?"

After a pause, Mercedes says, "If Hugh can see you half-naked, I suppose I'm allowed to help undress his friend."

"I heard that," Hugh says from the door.

"I meant for you to," Mercedes tosses back. They exchange a smile that confuses me.

"I can handle this on my own," Ashley says with a chuckle before meeting my gaze. Her expression softens. "I know you're not happy, but please don't try to kill me. All I'm going to do is clean you up a little."

I wince. "You're safe." The idea of her washing me down has my blood pumping, but sadly that only makes the pain in my head more excruciating.

"All set, Mercedes," Ashley says.

"You're sure?" Mercedes asks.

"She's sure," Hugh answers in a playful tone.

Ashley removes my shoes, slacks, jacket, and shirt, leaving me standing in my skivvies. She walks away and returns quickly with a cool, wet cloth that she runs over my face, neck, and hands. I stand and let her. Why?

Maybe because I'm struggling to believe this is happening.

Or maybe because her touch is as addictive as the sight of her.

I don't complain as she helps me onto her bed and covers me with a white cloud of softness. "Hey," I croak.

"Yes?" She hovers by the side of the bed.

I feel heavy. So heavy. I struggle to keep my eyes open as

I murmur, "Don't let them kill me in my sleep."

Her small hand closes around mine. "Rest and heal. You're safe. I promise."

I give into the pull of unconsciousness while clinging to the words I've waited my whole life to hear.

Chapter Four

Ashley

I DON'T HAVE the heart to let go of Ray's hand even after his eyes close. To say I'm in shock would be an understatement. The violence of the scene I just witnessed is only now beginning to sink in.

My mother is one of the strongest people I ever met and I'm grateful for so much of the advice she gave me over the years. I lost count of how many times she told me to hold myself together during a crisis . . . fear and tears are a luxury one allows only afterward. That's not just talk. She walks that walk. She started her career as an EMT to pay her way through school. Later, she worked as an RN in an emergency room as she continued her education. Her title may now be MD, but not much else has changed about her over the years.

The only person I know who doesn't admire her is my dumb-ass twin brother who took off to California to chase fame. We only hear from him when he needs money. Funny how two people can share a womb and childhood and turn out as different as he and I did.

I've decided he takes after our father. My mother doesn't like to talk about either one of them. She told me once that my father was a nice man who was looking for a nice woman—and made the mistake of falling for one who was too much for him to handle. They stayed together until my brother and I were born. He wanted to marry her, build her a nice house, and take care of her. She wanted to save the world one person at a time and preparing for something like that consumed so much of her time and energy that he gave her a choice: her dreams or him.

I know his name and his address. He found a woman who shared his idea of what a family should be and they have four beautiful children. For a while I stalked them on social media. He's a well-liked person working as a bank manager. His wife looks like a model and makes videos about their family life and how happy it is. She has an impressive online following.

I called him once because I wanted to meet my half-siblings. He begged me not to contact him again because his wife doesn't know about us and he thought our existence could disrupt his marriage.

I agree with my mother on many things, but not about my bio-father's character. There's nothing nice about that kind of weakness.

That one conversation explained everything I needed to

know about him and why he couldn't stay with my mother. I've seen my mother talk a weapon out of a drug addict's hands. I watched her pull over behind a car accident and calmly call for assistance before risking her life to comfort the trapped victims.

She *was* too much for him.

I'm glad she never let him convince her that was a bad thing.

So, yes, my head was still spinning from the things I was told by Mercedes and Cheryl as soon as we'd entered my apartment. Despite both Hugh and Jack being here, I can't say I believed they were super soldiers. And I would have bet my life that neither of them had ever been trapped in silverware.

I was impressed, however, by their commitment to the fantasy, especially when Hugh demanded to know where the knife was. I was amused that my role in their skit was the woman who'd chosen the one utensil that could endanger everyone.

I mean, who doesn't love a bad boy?

Nice wasn't good enough for my mother, and it sure as hell isn't what I want.

Not that I believed any of this was real.

Not even when Ray twisted Jack's head to the side and Jack hit the floor. I thought it was an act. Things like that don't happen. Horror set in when Ray essentially destroyed Hugh's body in front of us.

There was nothing fake about Mercedes' cries of fear.

Cheryl's reassurances that Hugh would heal were emotional.

These men are what they claim to be.

They have superhuman strength and their injuries heal with frightening speed.

The bed dips as Cheryl comes to sit on the edge of it near Ray's feet. Jack stands beside the bed, his clothing bloodied, but his wounds gone. She lets out a shaky sigh. "Well, that was terrifying."

I give Ray's hand a gentle squeeze. "For all involved."

She nods. "I'm sorry I went MIA. I should have told you about Jack, but . . ."

I look from her to him and back then let out an unamused laugh. "I wouldn't have believed you, so I get it."

Jack chimes in quietly. "What you saw doesn't represent who Ray is. I don't know what becoming a knife did to him, or if they gave him something that messed up his head, but that wasn't the Ray I know."

I gaze down at Ray's flushed face. His breathing is labored. His skin is burning hot. "He needs a doctor."

Jack shakes his head. "We can't risk that."

My eyes narrow and I shoot him a glare. "He could die."

Shifting from one foot to another, Jack shakes his head again. "I would give my life for him . . ."

"But . . ."

He glances at Cheryl and blinks. "This isn't just about

me. There may be nine more men trapped in that silverware. They can't be exposed before we have a chance to free them. Ray wouldn't want us to choose him over them."

"After what just went down in my office, I have serious doubts you have any idea what Ray would want."

"Ray has risked his life over much less." Jack pockets his hands. "Like I said, that wasn't him. We're brothers. We stand and fight as one—"

"Or fall and die together. Yeah, I heard you say that, but I don't see you willing to die for Ray, and Hugh certainly isn't. So, hop down off that soapbox and do something for your friend here."

Jack's expression tightens. "If I knew what to do, don't you think I would already be doing it?"

Cheryl stands and joins him, wrapping her arms around his waist. "Ashley, we're just worried. Someone has been following us. Jack noticed someone watching us the other day then someone followed me earlier. That's why I was so late to meet you."

"Who?"

"We don't know," Cheryl says. "When they realized I knew they were tailing me, they took off. It may seem that Hugh doesn't care about Ray, but he planned to bring Ray back . . . just not yet. You saw for yourself how dangerous Ray can be. All Hugh wanted was time to wake the others first."

I meet Jack's tormented gaze. "You didn't agree with that

plan."

He takes a moment to answer. "I don't handle being a spoon as well as Hugh handles being a fork. For me, it's a prison. I can sense Cheryl, but I can't free myself and that's... unsettling. From what I know of Ray's life before Inkwell, being trapped and helpless would be torture and I couldn't do that to him."

"But you can sit back now and let him die? I don't understand the rules of this *brotherhood*."

"Ashley—" Cheryl begins.

"No," I cut in. "I want to hear it from Jack. Are you loyal only until it threatens you and what you care about? If so, that's not loyalty. What happened to the fall and die together? Too much commitment for a *spoon* to handle?"

Jack sucks in an audible breath. After a moment, he says, "Ray's here so Hugh's plan is already not an option. But if we take Ray to a hospital and they run bloodwork on him... we might as well call the government and tell them to come get him as well as the rest of us because that's what they'll do."

That's a good point. "Okay, so we need a doctor but one we can trust. I have one of those."

Cheryl straightens and her eyes widen. "Your mother? Are you sure you want to involve her? This situation is extremely dangerous."

"Do you have a better idea?"

Her lips press together and it's clear she doesn't.

I release Ray's hand and reach for my phone. "Mom, I need you. I'm at my apartment. Could you come here, bring your medical bag, and not tell anyone where you're going?"

"Anything specific I should prepare for?"

I give her a quick rundown of Ray's symptoms. I also explain that taking him to urgent care or a hospital is not currently possible.

"On my way," my mother says before ending the call.

I toss my phone on the bed in front of me and reclaim Ray's hand. The odd connection I felt to the knife is still there and even stronger now that he's in human form. This is the man who called to me and I answered by taking him home.

I glance at Jack. "Were either you or Hugh sick when you came back?"

"No. Confused—yes. Sick? Not at all."

"Earlier, you said you'd all agreed to not take those drugs anymore. What drugs were you referring to?"

From the doorway, Hugh says, "They never told us what was in them, but taking them was a requirement for being in the program. At first, we thought they were meant to help us handle the injections better, but they were more than that. On them, we could go for days without sleeping. That concerned me, but what made me stop taking them was when several men in our unit began to have unprovoked fits of rage. They were removed and never seen again. Those of us who remained began to covertly throw the pills away."

"Except Ray." Jack looks down at his friend sadly. "And I understood. Withdrawing from the drug was temporarily worse than staying on it. We lost a few more good men to madness. They were taken away as well."

"Taken away where? By who?"

For a moment there's such sadness in Jack's expression that I regret asking. There's a huge difference between imagining an evil organization experimenting on faceless soldiers nearly a century ago and hearing about those atrocities from someone who survived it.

"Whoever Director Falcon worked for, at least, that was our guess. You must understand that Project Inkwell worked in the shadows of the military. On paper and for the purpose of history, we died before the war. Our families believed that. Falcon told us we'd all someday go home after the war, but I don't know that any of us truly believed that. You don't send dead men back to their families—not men like us. We're the secrets governments dispose of."

Hugh adds, "We traded our souls for the chance to be more than we were."

Jack exchanges a look with Hugh. Something tells me he held out hope for a loophole to that deal. I go over the events they outlined when we'd first entered my apartment. "So, you were all invited to an award dinner. Ray met with your director before it began and can't remember anything after that."

"According to him," Hugh says.

Jack puffs. "He has no reason to lie." I like him more every time he defends Ray.

Hugh shrugs. "Unless he does."

This isn't getting us anywhere. "My mother will be here soon. Is there anything you know that can help her treat him?"

Jack and Hugh exchange another look before Jack says, "Ray is a good man, but is that still him? We don't know what they gave him or if it broke him."

It saddens me to imagine the kind of evil that could not only create these men, but then callously erase them when they were deemed no longer useful. Every life has value and is worth fighting for. "I'm not asking you about his character; I'm asking what you think he needs medically."

"I don't know," Hugh answers. "But whatever happens, you have to keep his heart pumping. We heal—fast, but only if we're alive."

As overwhelming as all of this is, it's also fascinating. "Like a starfish."

"But faster," Jack adds.

"Sea cucumbers can regenerate their gut and enteric nervous system." I glance down at Ray and gasp. "He's as white as my sheets. Is he dying?" His hand is still warm in mine. I reach up to touch his forehead—still hot.

"Hugh can match any background he touches," Mercedes says cheerfully. "Like an octopus."

Like an octopus. I wouldn't have believed that was possible an hour ago, but I wasn't sure what to believe about anything anymore. "What kind of multicellular sea creature cocktail injection did they give you?"

Jack shrugs uncomfortably. "We weren't exactly in a situation where we could ask a lot of questions."

A heavy silence follows. Ray's labored breathing intensifies. From head to toe, his body begins to shake and I've never felt more helpless. I lean over and speak softly in his ear. "Don't you dare give up, Ray. You destroyed my office. Your ass needs to stick around to help me fix it. I'm not losing my deposit over this." Ray doesn't wake, but his lips twitch slightly as if he can hear me and is amused.

"Your mother's here!" Cheryl announces.

I reluctantly straighten and stand. The speed at which my mother's eyes dart around the room is the only sign that the blood-covered office she just walked by affected her. I'm the first one she assesses. Relieved that I appear unharmed, she quickly scans the others. Her eyes widen slightly as she seems to note the lack of injuries beneath the bloodied clothing.

I rush to her side and give her a quick hug. She returns it, but I can tell she's already in emergency doctor mode. Without hesitation, I update her on Ray's symptoms.

After giving everyone in the room one last long look, she turns her attention to Ray. "How long has he been like this?"

"Thirty-ish minutes," I reply.

The look she shoots me is one I know. My mother

doesn't deal in approximations. She wants detailed and accurate information.

"Is it substance-induced?" she asks.

"We believe so." I chew my bottom lip. "But there are extenuating circumstances that you need to be aware of."

She places her large medical bag on the side of the bed next to Ray's arm and leans closer to study his pale skin. His arm's color changes to match the print of her bag. I know the second she sees it happen because her eyes rivet to mine. "Ashley Anne, what am I dealing with here?"

Oh, crap, she just middle-named me. I take a deep breath and gush, "A World War II super soldier the government tried to erase when the war ended but accidentally turned into silverware. He's the third to revert to human form. We believe dopamine and testosterone is what the first two use to initiate the transformation. Ray appears to have come back on his own but possibly due to a drug he may have been given right before the attempted erasure."

My mother pins me with a look.

I've never lied to her, never even been one to make up stories. "And the others?" she demands.

"You know Cheryl," I say breathlessly.

"Hello, Cheryl," my mother says as if this is the most normal situation in the world.

"Hi, Ashley's mom," Cheryl says. She takes Jack by the arm. "This is my . . . we're . . . This is Jack."

"I'm Mercedes," Mercedes chirps happily. "And this is

Hugh. We're engaged. He was a fork. Sometimes he still is. It's complicated."

My mother nods slowly. "I see."

Mercedes continues, "Jack was a spoon."

"Are you all super soldiers?"

I wince as Mercedes doesn't seem to hear the sarcasm in my mother's tone. She answers in a gush, "A super soldier? Me?" Mercedes laughs. "I wish. No, Cheryl and I are just the women who discovered how to bring these men back."

My mother frowns. "And how is that?"

Mercedes smile widens. "Let's just say it requires having an intimate knowledge of silverware."

Nope, my mother is not amused. There's enough destruction in my office, though, that she is willing to entertain the ramblings of those she considers mentally unstable long enough to learn what happened. I've seen her use the same technique in the ER.

Her attention returns to me and her eyebrows rise in her signature expression that tells me she and I will have a long and serious talk as soon as she can get me alone.

I feel the need to clarify and raise both of my hands in a plea for her to believe me. "I don't know anything about that part. Ray was already in human form when I got home."

"He entered your apartment without your knowledge?" Her eyes narrow.

"I brought him here, but I didn't know any of this was real."

She searches my face. "Did you take something also?"

I shake my head vehemently. "Of course not."

Ray's breathing becomes louder and my mother loses interest in what I'm saying as her attention returns to him. She checks his eyes and his pulse, her movements becoming more controlled as she assesses the seriousness of his condition. "Call an ambulance. He needs a crash unit. Now."

"Mom, you don't understand—"

"Now!" she repeats herself forcefully and gives me a look so full of disappointment I'm shaken to the core. She's never looked at me that way before.

When she turns back to Ray he's gone. "Where did he go?"

I lean closer. There, mostly tucked beneath my comforter, is a knife. He's a knife again. This is real. Ray's a knife. I knew it, but now that I've seen it—Holy shit. "He reverted back to knife form."

My mother blinks a few times quickly before she looks around the room again. "I don't know what's going on here, but you clearly think I have more of a sense of humor than I do. Regardless of how elaborate of a prank you create, I will never find a potentially life-threatening event amusing."

I touch her arm, trying to reach her with more than my words. "Mom, this isn't a joke. I don't do pranks or drugs. And when have you known me to fabricate something as wild as this?"

She inhales and looks skyward as if requesting patience.

"Well, you have named the robots you work on and refer to them as your friends."

I wave that off. "Outside of that."

Mercedes pipes in, "If it helps, Hugh could change back into a fork."

"I could," he says with a nod.

Cheryl shakes her head. "That wasn't enough to convince me. I thought it was some kind of magic trick."

My mother picks up her bag. "As entertaining as you all hoped this would be, I have an early shift tomorrow and my time would be better spent resting this evening." She glances over her shoulder. "I hope you have something that will get whatever you used for blood out of the rug."

I grab her arm. "Don't go, Mom." I look in the direction of the knife. "You have to be here when he comes back." A depressing thought comes to me. "*If* he comes back. Do you think he's dead?"

"The *knife*?"

I nod.

My mother bends down, pulls back the comforter, and places a finger across the part of the knife where the handle meets the blade. "No pulse. Cold. I'm confident in my call that this utensil is not alive."

When she straightens, I meet her gaze. "This isn't a joke, Mom. The man you just saw is in that knife."

She shakes her head in disgust. "Then you need a plan for when he comes back because whoever was here was doing a realistic impression of a dying man."

"It wasn't an impression. He might be withdrawing from a drug the government gave him."

She rubs a hand across her forehead. "Ashley, I love you, but I am not sitting on a large amount of money. If you're trying to put me into a mental hospital to gain access to my estate, you'll sadly discover I owe enough in college loans that I'll still be paying them from the grave."

I glance around, hoping someone else has a way to convince her. I wouldn't have believed this story either if I hadn't seen the men tearing each other apart and healing almost as quickly as they broke. "How can I prove that they're super soldiers? What if I cut one of them right now and you see for yourself how quickly they heal."

Jack murmured, "That wouldn't be my first choice of how to convince her. Let's just show her this—" In front of our eyes he becomes a spoon that clatters to the floor.

This time my mother's expression becomes distressed. "Are you also drugging me? Ashley, I've shown you what effects psychedelic substances can have on the brain. It's nothing you should ever expose someone to and especially not without their consent. How are you administering it? Aerosol form? Was it on something I touched? How much was the dose? Oh, Ashley, this was so careless . . ."

I take her bag from her, then enclose both of her hands in mine. "You're not being drugged, Mom. This is real. These men were governmental experiments and the one on my bed was given something that might kill him if he returns. I need your help. Ray needs your help. I'm the one who brought him back. I'm responsible. We must save him, Mom, and you're the only one I trust enough to do it. So, put aside your doubts, or play along with this, but please—I'm begging you. Help me save him."

No one speaks or moves for a long moment. Eventually, my mother inhales deeply and looks at the knife on the bed again. She's not convinced, but she's concerned enough to play along again. "If any of this were true, I suppose the first step would be to identify what your friend was given. For that, I would need a blood sample. But how to get one from an inanimate object is beyond my expertise."

"I'm covered with his blood," Hugh says as he holds one bloodied arm up. "It could be mine, no, that's definitely Ray's. It's also all over my sleeve."

With a forced smile, my mother says, "Delightful."

I shake her arm, "But could you use it to run some tests? Would that be enough to determine what they gave him?"

She's confused, but at least she no longer thinks I'm drugging her. "It might be."

"Give me your shirt, Hugh," I demand. He sheds it and hands it to me. I hold it out to my mother. "How long would the tests take you?"

"If I do them myself?"

"You'd have to. No one can know about this."

"Because?"

"This is about more than the three men in this room . . ."

My mother cocks an eyebrow and I know what she's thinking: Currently, there is one man, a spoon and a knife, but this isn't the time to focus on semantics. She knows what I mean.

In a gravelly voice, Hugh says, "There are twelve of us. At least, there were. We have someone following us. Who? We don't know, but we're potentially already in danger. All that matters right now, though, is saving Ray. Tell me what you require as proof that we are who we say we are. I can become a fork in front of you, but you'll only see that as another trick. I can slice my arm and let you watch it heal in real time. I have a long list of things I regret. I refuse to add Ray's death to it. What can I do to get you to help us?"

Now, it might have been because Hugh is a gorgeous, half-naked man with beautiful eyes, but my mother nods. "I'll run tests on the blood on your shirt. I can't make any promises and it may take me a few hours, but if I find anything useful, I'll be back."

"Thank you," Hugh says in a deep voice and my mother's face flushes. Really? All it took was a muscled chest for all her disbelief to melt away?

"He's engaged, Mom," I murmur as I usher her out of the bedroom, down the hall, past my war-torn office, and to the door.

She shoots me a look so stern that under any other circumstance I would have laughed. Under all that seriousness, she's still a woman who isn't immune to a strong man. None of that is important right now, though. "What should I do if he comes back while you're gone?"

"You mean if he changes from a knife into a man again?"

"Yes."

She opens her mouth to say something, seems to change her mind, then says, "Without knowing what he's on, I can't say. My suggestion? Make sure he stays a knife until we have more information."

Make sure he stays a knife?

How the hell do I do that?

I didn't bring him back the first time.

Chapter Five

Ray

I'M IN LIMBO again. At least I'm not in pain.

I'd wonder if I'm dead, but something tells me I'm not lucky enough to be.

She's with me. Ashley. I feel her presence and her warmth.

I should be angry. Hugh and Jack just tried to kill me. I don't crave revenge—I crave her.

Memories of her keep the darker ones at bay. I don't believe in religion or an afterlife, but she could convince me that angels exist. Fierce. Protective. Caring. If there is someone watching over us, I'd be disappointed if they were anything else.

And beautiful.

She's so fucking beautiful.

A man could fill his home with paintings of a woman like her. She could grace the hallway, claim the wall over the fireplace, fill every frame on every shelf. I doubt I could tire of her image.

It's been years since I've had sex... shit, according to her well over eighty years...

It could be that I'm hungry for any female companionship and this one just happened to flash me her tits. No, our connection feels deeper than that.

She's calling me back to her.

A beacon through the darkness.

I couldn't resist her even if I wanted to. I give myself over to the desire to be with her again.

This time when I drop, it's onto my back and the softness of a bed. Her hand closes around mine and I smile because nothing has ever felt so right. Pain begins to nip at me, but I ignore it and turn my head toward her. She's even more beautiful than I remember. "Ashley," my voice is raspy.

Her hand tightens on mine. "How do you feel?"

I struggle to sit up and am surprised by how weak I am. "Not as good as I'm used to." I remember the last thing I said to her and joke, "Thank you for not letting them kill me."

She grazes the side of my face lightly with her free hand. "They weren't trying to kill you. All they wanted was for you to stay a knife until they knew what to do with you."

"Stay a knife? Oh, yes, you said my unit was changed into silverware. Is that the story you're holding to?"

A smile thins her lips. "I have a robust imagination, but I couldn't make this shit up. And before you tell me what an unbelievable story it is, I'm not the one who changes color to match my environment. I have so many questions about what they injected you with, but our first priority is to make sure you don't die."

My usual response to that would be an offhand: "Death is the goal—but not *today's* goal." Outside of my work for Inkwell, I had nothing to live for. I don't feel that way when I look into Ashley's eyes.

She's not just beautiful—she's kind.

Brave.

Mine.

I shake my head and regret that move instantly when everything blurs and it feels like someone is using a sledgehammer on my forehead. "Thank you," is all I can muster.

"It's possible someone slipped something into the drink you had before the award dinner. My working theory is whatever it was had dopamine in it because neither Hugh nor Jack can come back without being intimate with a woman. You don't require that."

"Sorry." I attempt charm as she comes back into focus.

Her smile widens.

Amazing how little everything else matters when she looks at me. I've never felt so greedy to have more of someone. The temptation to pull her forward and across my chest is strong. All that holds me back is the uncertainty of accidentally hurting her. I wasn't the only man in the unit who unintentionally hurt people before I understood how strong

I'd become. Even shaking someone's hand was an act that required restraint. The men in my unit disagreed many times over the years, but never about the importance of protecting innocents from injury. Women were off limits until we were sure being with them would be safe.

Where had this woman come from? And why did Hugh and Jack both have a woman? "Are you a prostitute?" I ask.

Her mouth drops open then presses into a straight line. "And if I am?"

I lift a shoulder in a shrug but regret it as a sharp pain shoots through me. "I don't judge a person for doing whatever they need to do to survive."

Her eyes soften and she takes my hand again. "That's such a good answer, I almost forgive you for questioning my occupation."

Another wave of pain cuts through me and I do my best to keep my face expressionless. I sigh in relief as it abates.

Seemingly unaware of my struggle, she says, "I'm a research analyst, thank you for asking."

She's adorable. "I didn't, but I should have. What does a research analyst do?"

"That completely depends on what field they work in."

I bring her hand to my chest and lay it flat over my heart. "You. What do *you* do?"

Her voice is breathless when she answers. "I work for a small robotics company. Originally, I was hired to crunch market data, but I love to work with the robots and they seem to genuinely enjoy spending time with me."

"Robots . . . because I'm in the future?" I tug her a little closer, until her hip is against the side of my leg. Ah, heaven.

"You don't believe it?"

I shrug. Honestly, I don't know what's real and what's not. All of this could be a dream or a hallucination. It feels jumbled enough to be either. I'm half expecting someone to kick me in the ribs to wake me and tell me I'm late to my meeting with Director Falcon.

Both of my legs cramp painfully and I sit straight up. Okay, that doesn't feel like a dream. The muscles in my chest contract as well and for a moment I can't get air into my lungs. I fight to inhale but nothing happens.

"Breathe," she says.

Trying, I think, but couldn't say it even if I wanted to.

The pain shifts, air fills my lungs and I collapse backward onto the bed, shaking from head to toe. The temperature in the room begins to lower. I close my eyes briefly. Cold. So fucking cold.

"Don't you dare die, Ray. All you have to do is hang on until my mother gets back and she'll save you. She's amazing."

I force my eyes open and attempt to look calm despite the realization that this might be the day I die. "Tell me about your robots."

She takes out a small device. It displays little color photos of tiny machines about the size of a child's baby doll. Each machine is dressed like a person, some with hats. One is in a suit and tie, but the suit has three arms because the robot does. "They're all failed prototypes that were headed toward the scrap pile, but I asked if I could use them to test the durability of materials. Dressing them up is just a hobby of mine but no one makes a big deal about it because . . . I work with mostly men and they like me."

"That's easy to believe."

She stops and smiles at me before continuing. "Can I trust you with a secret?"

"I promise to take it to my grave." It was an easy promise to make considering it didn't feel like I was going to survive the day.

"I took advantage of the access I had. I couldn't help myself, the robots looked so sad. I researched what the code equivalent to dopamine would be for a machine and wrote a few lines into their BIOS. Everyone deserves to feel good now and then, right? It also made them more eager to perform tasks." Her mouth rounds. "Oh, my God, the drugs they gave you . . . did they make you feel good?"

"Absolutely."

"And would you say . . . more likely to follow orders without questioning them?"

My level of pain is increasing and my muscles are now spasming beyond what I can conceal, so it's a struggle to focus on what she's saying, but I do my best to. "Yes. I'd say they did, but they also brought on fits of rage."

She looks down at her little device and taps on it with her fingers. "That information might be helpful to my mother."

"Is that a communication device? Like a radio?"

"It's a telephone and a computer. It's attached to the internet . . . the internet is . . ."

I half-listen to her explanation while fighting panic each time it becomes difficult to breathe. The room keeps getting colder, but I suspect the issue is with me and not the thermometer. My teeth begin to chatter.

"He's awake," I hear Jack say. I don't try to sit up or greet him. There isn't an inch of me that isn't in agony. "How's he—oh, shit, he doesn't look good."

"Thanks," I croak out.

"Hugh," Jack calls out. *Great. That's exactly what I need.* I grunt. Imagine if that's the last face I see before I go to the light.

"How long has he been back?" Hugh demands.

Nice to see you too, I think.

"Maybe fifteen minutes," Ashley says. "I've been trying to keep him calm."

Jack asks, "Have you heard from your mother?"

"She's on her way back—about ten minutes out."

As optimistic as ever, Hugh says, "He'll be dead by then."

Ashley touches my cheek gently. "You can't stay here, Ray. My mother isn't back yet. Go to wherever you were."

A heaviness begins to spread through me but I fight it. Thinking clearly becomes more difficult. "I don't want to go back."

She leans closer, so close her breath warms my cheek. "You have to. You're sick. My mother will be here soon with something to help you. You just have to hold on."

Breathing is a struggle and the temperature of the room takes another quick dive. "I want to stay with you."

"You can't."

Her image blurs. There is only pain and an increasing difficulty to breathe. "I belong here—with you."

I can't see him, but I hear Jack say, "You need to make him want to go." Jack leans down over me, his face filling my vision. "You need to go back to being a knife, Ray. It's the only way you'll survive this."

Between clenched teeth, I demand, "How the fuck do I do that?"

Ashley's hand closes around mine again. "He's right. Whatever you did to come here, do the reverse. You can do this."

"You have to do this," Jack affirms.

I search their faces, then settle on Ashley's concerned one. I wish I could do what they're asking me to, but I don't know how. As I look into those beautiful eyes of hers, I don't want to leave. If I do die, at least I'll die holding the hand of the only person I ever felt really saw me. She does. I can tell. She doesn't see the angry, wild child I was or the broken young man my father created. She's not afraid of what I've become. She sees *me* and I don't want to go back without her.

My chest tightens again.

Pain rocks through me.

Everything blurs.

But I cling to her. For the first time in my life, I don't feel alone and I don't care if holding onto that feeling costs me everything.

"Let go of his hand," Hugh growls.

Ashley's grip on me doesn't lessen. "No. He needs me."

Hugh physically breaks our connection and if I had the strength I would kill him right now. I don't though. I don't even have the oxygen to voice how much I hate him. "What he needs is to become a knife again until your mother gets back. Do you want to comfort him or do you want him to live, because you can't have both."

"I want him to live," Ashley says in a small voice that makes me not want to go even more. She's hurting. I need to stay and protect her.

"Then get out of this room," Hugh orders. "Now."

Every cell in me mourns the loss of her and my rage at Hugh gives me the strength to not only sit up, but to leap to my feet on the bed. Okay, so my body is shutting down. Fine. I'll die, but I'm taking Hugh with me.

I lunge at him.

He steps back and catches me as my momentum would

have landed me on the floor. In my ear, he growls, "Go back to the void, Ray. You think she cares about you? She's not real. How could she be? No one wants you here. No one ever did. No one ever will. Nothingness is better than this illusion. Go back."

And just like that I'm alone again.

Physically pain-free, but hurting in a way that is so much worse.

Chapter Six

Ashley

I STAND OUTSIDE the door of my bedroom and pray I made the right decision. Mercedes hugs me and I tell her I'm fine, but I'm not. What if Ray dies without me there? Was I right? Wrong?

Hugh appears at the door and I hold my breath. His eyes are dark and pained. Oh, God. "Is Ray . . .?"

"He's a knife again," Hugh says coldly and walks past me. "Don't go in there until your mother gets here."

I wipe a tear from my cheek and look up to see Jack. His expression is taut. "Was he still alive when he changed back into a knife?" I have to ask . . . I have to know.

He nods slowly. Cheryl appears and hugs Jack. Only then does he meet my gaze. "Hugh might have just saved Ray's life, but I hate there wasn't another way. Ray deserves happiness just as much, if not more, than the rest of us do. It's not right that this is how he comes back." He inhales and closes his eyes briefly before meeting my gaze again. "I don't understand how this works or why our connection is so strong to the people who bring us back, but you matter to Ray. If he does survive this, that feeling will only get stronger the more time he spends with you."

I half joke, "You say that like it's a bad thing."

"It could be—if you don't feel the same. He set out to save the world, but he'd burn it down for someone he loves."

I swallow hard. That's a little terrifying, but I'm not going to lie, also exciting. "Love? He barely knows me."

"He chose you." Jack kisses the top of Cheryl's head. "Once that happens, nothing matters more than that bond. Nothing."

I think back to how Jack stood up for Ray until Hugh brought Cheryl's welfare into the equation. She's looking up at him with so much love it's obvious that feeling goes both ways.

Could Ray and I have that?

I feel for him—but more than I would for anyone I witnessed struggling to survive? I don't know. "I'll be careful," I say.

Beside me, Mercedes gushes, "This part is tough, but think of how amazing everything will soon be. We're manifesting an adventure unlike anything I'm sure any of us allowed ourselves to believe we could have."

How can she always be so fucking happy? Is she completely oblivious to Hugh's suffering? "Read the room, Mercedes. None of us would choose this *adventure*."

She glances over her shoulder in the direction Hugh went. "That's because you've been fed the lie that good things are supposed to come easily. There's nothing easy about making a good life for yourself or in loving someone. I know Hugh well enough to know that he just did something he didn't want to, but he did it because he felt he had to. I could go tell him it's okay, but that wouldn't help. He needs a moment because if I go to him now, he'll feel that he has to pretend he's okay for me. He does better when he comes to me. I'm the opposite, I don't want to be alone when I'm hurting. But loving someone means accepting that they don't have to be exactly like you. They can be beautifully different."

Cheryl looks at Mercedes. "So, you're afraid of saying something to him that'll make things worse?"

Mercedes wrinkles her nose. "That too."

I nod. I get it. I have no idea what I'd say to him either. Had I stayed with Ray, there's a very good chance he might not have changed back into a knife and that could have cost him his life. Still, I can't help but hate Hugh a little for tearing my hand from Ray's and sending me out of the room. I also can't help hating myself a little for going. I don't want to admit it, but Mercedes is making a lot of sense lately. I do want good things to come easily. I don't want the difficult path to be the right one.

Hugh probably feels the same way.

As I rewind the last few minutes and go over them again,

my anger with him dissolves. "Please tell Hugh that I appreciate what he did and how hard it must have been for him."

Mercedes hugs me again before saying, "Now that's something I know he needs to hear." With that, she walks away to find him.

"What do we do now?" Cheryl asks.

"We wait," I answer then look down at my phone to track my mother's location. "Five more minutes."

Five minutes never felt so long.

I meet my mother at the door and fill her in on what happened while she was gone—not what was said or how anyone felt—only the facts. "Do you have something that can help him?"

She pauses mid-stride and pins me with a look. "I was able to study not only his blood but also some skin samples that were on Hugh's shirt. I didn't believe you until I looked at both under a microscope. His blood cells are enlarged and uniquely shaped. There was a high presence of white blood cells that were still active. All of it, including his skin cells, had metallic inclusions, some kind of organic/inorganic structure I've never seen before."

"Because he's sometimes a knife."

She shakes her head in bemusement. "His cell structure supports that possibility. Who are these men, Ashley? Hugh's shirt contained more than just Ray's blood so I tested it all. They're not human."

"They were. I told you, the government experimented on them. I've been going over and over what I've learned about them, and I think the injections they were given included DNA from Cephalopods, Echinoderm, and Holothurians."

"I wasn't able to study their DNA, but that would also explain why Ray can camouflage himself to match his surroundings."

"What I don't understand is if he can regenerate, why isn't Ray able to beat whatever drug they gave him? He almost died again. What would do that?"

"Using the blood samples from the other men, I was able to determine a baseline for what should show up and what Ray might have ingested. His HVA is extremely high, but his blood, unlike that of the others, contained a high amount of lead as well as biomarkers that indicate some other form of toxin. I hate making any conclusions based on rushed testing, but my guess is that they gave him some kind of domoic acid, possibly from algae, along with a bacterium designed to spike a fever." She looks skyward as she thinks.

I take a wild guess at where her thoughts are going. "An octopus's metabolic processes can be affected by extreme changes in temperature."

Her eyes light with pride. "A double punch. You weaken the immune system with poison, then set it on fire with a fever. The white cells would be produced exponentially until his system essentially turns on itself."

"It's a theory."

"So, what do we do?"

She laughs without humor. "I'm going to gamble that my instincts are right and give him an insanely high dose of antibiotics."

"Enough to knock out the fever."

"Or kill him." She shakes her head. "There are so many unknown variables . . ."

My mother doesn't say things like that lightly. She means it. "If you don't feel comfortable giving him the antibiotics, Mom, I will. We're his only chance."

"I'll do it, but I wish I could consult with a diagnostic team on this. I understand why these men have to remain off the radar, though. They're someone's mistake and would either be studied in a lab or terminated. When will governments learn to respect nature? Someone was playing God, and that never works out."

Hugh and Jack join us. "So? Do we have a plan?" Hugh asks.

I meet Mercedes' gaze from across the room and rush to Hugh, hugging him tightly. "We do and because of you, we might be able to save Ray."

Hugh's arms hover above me without touching me, but the shudder I feel pass through him tells me my words affected him. I release him and step back. He clears his throat. "Okay, so let's do this."

All of us gather around my bed where Ray, still in knife form, is laid out on the pillow. I desperately want him to live, but I don't know how to bring him back. Even if it's necessary, with my nerves jumbled as they are, I couldn't feel less like diddling a knife.

Not with everyone in the room.

Especially not with my mother there.

"Do you need a moment with him?" she asks and I cringe.

"Do you have ice cream?" Mercedes interjects.

Cheryl places a hand on my shoulder. "If your dopamine theory is correct, and if whatever they gave him included a dose of it, maybe all you have to do is touch him. He came back for you before. Just hold him in your hand. Tell him you care about him. Call him back to you."

I search the faces of Hugh and Jack. "Will he be able to hear me?"

Jack answers, "He'll know you're with him. I can't hear words when I'm a spoon, but I can feel Cheryl's presence, her touch . . . and when she yearns for me."

"It's the same for me and Mercedes," Hugh adds quietly.

I look down at the knife. I don't know him well enough to *yearn* for him. I do want to save him, though. I sit on the bed and lay my hand over the knife. "Ray, we're all here waiting for you. Come back."

The knife is cold beneath my touch and tears prick my eyes. I'd ask the others if they think he's still in there, but there's no way for them to know.

Mercedes sits beside me. "The scariest part of loving

someone is believing that you deserve to be happy and loved. Once you remove that block, everything changes. And it's magical."

I huff out a breath. "So, all I have to do is believe? Sorry, this isn't like making a wish over a birthday cake."

She tips her head toward one raised shoulder. "Or maybe, it's exactly like that. When we were kids, we still believed our dreams could come true. Maybe that kind of faith in things working out has an effect on if they do. You don't have to say anything you don't mean, but tell him how you feel. Tell him what you want. Let him hear you, feel you, and answer you."

I turn and meet my mother's gaze. Her lips spread in a kind smile. "If you're asking me if this is batshit crazy, it absolutely is. People becoming silverware? That wouldn't even make a good plot for a movie. But if you're asking me if I think you can bring him back, then you should know that I don't have a shred of doubt that you can. You are an incredible young woman and he'd be a fool to not come running back to you."

"Do knives run?" I ask with humor and a sniff. Having her here with me means more than I can ever express in words.

"Stop stalling." One eyebrow arches. "But if you decide to do more than hold him, warn me so I can step out of the room."

"That won't be necessary," I assure her, although I'm not

sure what I'm doing. I return my attention to the knife. "Just like making a wish on cake . . ." I run my fingers down the length of him then close my eyes. *I want you to live, Ray. I want good things to happen for you. I don't know if we're meant to be together or if I'm only meant to save you, but I want the chance to explore what could be—with you. Me and you, together. Let's do this. Let's save you, save your unit, and maybe fall in love along the way.*

At first there's nothing, then the knife begins to warm beneath my hand. He knows I'm here. I not only feel him, I feel his pain. He doesn't want to come back.

Tears fill my eyes. *Hugh didn't mean whatever he said to you, Ray. He wants you back, just like I do. So does Jack.*

So much pain. So much yearning. My heart is breaking for him.

I open my eyes. "I can't do this alone. Hugh. Jack. He needs you too." They both give me an odd look. "Put your hands on him next to mine." When neither move to do it, I say more forcefully, "Get your asses over here. You sent him back. He needs to hear from you as well."

I move my hand to the middle of the knife. Jack walks to the other side of the bed, sits, and lays his hand on the handle of the knife. Hugh moves to an open space beside me, sits and places his hand on the remaining part.

As if I know what I'm doing, I tell them both to close their eyes. "Hugh, tell him why you did what you did. And Jack, tell him how much you love Cheryl and why you felt leaving him in the knife was the only way you could protect her. Let him know that he matters to you and that your plan was always to save him."

Only after they both close their eyes do I do the same. *Ray, listen to me... listen to them. You're not alone. We're right here waiting for you. Come back to us.*

When the knife begins to vibrate, Hugh says, "I'm out." And steps away.

Jack breaks his connection as well.

I hold on and trust that even if Ray can't hear me, he can feel my emotions because I can feel his. He's afraid, but not so afraid that he doesn't want to come back. He's been hurt and he thinks that whatever was done to him was somehow his fault. *It wasn't, Ray. Bad things happen to good people. But good things can happen as well. Come back.*

He vibrates again.

I keep my eyes closed. *You need to know you matter to someone. I understand that. I need the same thing. Will that be you? I can't promise you forever if you won't give us a chance to get to know each other first. But I need to be loved as much as you do. Is that what you want to hear? I crave belonging to someone too. I know what it's like to not be important to someone who should love me, but you know what? The people who don't love me don't define me. It's the people who do who matter.*

Don't leave me hanging here, Ray.
My mother's watching.

Side note, she won't be easy to win over, but if you treat me well, she's also the type who'd burn down the world for the people she loves.

Just like me.

But you won't ever know what it's like to have us on your side if you don't come back.

Chapter Seven

Ray

As soon my back hits the softness of the bed, I jolt to a seated position and reach for Ashley's hand. I don't understand how we communicate without words; however, I feel what she's feeling.

Her fingers lace with mine and her smile is teary. "You came back."

"I always will—for you." No words ring truer to me. We spend several long moments simply looking into each other's eyes.

"And I thought it was for me," Hugh jokes in the background.

"Fuck you," I say, but there's no bite to my tone. I'd like to think I would have returned without him, but when he'd reached out to me while I was ... wherever I was ... I *felt* his regret and his commitment to save me. A spoken apology would never have moved me the way that fleeting connection did.

We exchange a quick look before I seek out Jack. He always said he cared about me, but I never really believed him. When we connected, I felt his love for me. He sees me as a brother, just as he always claimed to.

He loves Cheryl... in a different way, but she means just as much to him. I don't know how they came to be, but I understand they are bonded now. She's his and he's hers. He couldn't choose me over her and I wouldn't want him to.

We exchange a nod.

"We don't have time for this." An older version of Ashley steps closer to the bed with a clear bag of liquid in one hand. I vaguely remember her from earlier. This is Ashley's mother.

In an authoritative tone, she says, "Ray, I'm going to put an IV in your arm. This is a high dose of antibiotics. We need to get it into you before your body begins to battle itself again."

Ashley releases my hand then stands to get out of the way. "Okay, Ray?"

I put my arm out. "Do it."

A moment later, there's a needle in one arm and a bag hung from the bedpost. Ashley's mother checks my eyes, pulse, and temperature. As if she were discussing the weather, she says, "Ray, my name is Lauren. If you start to feel cold, tell me." She takes out a needle and withdraws blood from my other arm.

When her mother steps away to put the vial of blood into a bag, Ashley sits near me, close enough that I can feel the warmth emanating from her body, but she's still too far away. I shift my weight and she slides toward me, her thigh coming to rest against mine.

"Smooth," she says lightly.

I shoot her a wink. "You have no idea."

"How do you feel?" she asks.

"Surprisingly, not shitty."

We link hands again. "I hope this works."

"Me too."

The room falls silent. Hugh wraps his arms around Mercedes from behind. Jack pulls Cheryl to his side and hugs her. Ashley's mother returns to stand next to the bed. All eyes are on me. They're waiting for a sign that I'm either getting better or worse.

I am as well.

In the past, I would have said I didn't care either way, but I was given a second chance. Why? I have no idea. But, despite everything I went through, I'm still here.

Ashley's hand finds mine again and I smile at her. She's why I'm here. This beautiful, brave woman. She doesn't have as much faith in us as I do, but that's okay. We are destined to be together. I don't mind if it takes time to convince her of that.

"I might not die," I say lightly.

"Too soon for that joke to be funny," she answers with a small smile.

Her mother takes my pulse and temperature again. "Your

pulse is steady. No fever."

I flex the hand with the finger that had struggled to heal. No pain. Full range of motion. "I think it's working."

Ashley scans my face. "The first two times, you seemed to get progressively worse the longer you were here. Do you feel anything odd at all?"

I frown. "There is something."

Her mouth parts. "What?"

I lean up and claim her mouth with mine and don't care that we have an audience. She feels as essential to my survival as air. And the kiss? I keep it gentle, but I don't want to. I crave her to the point it's painful.

Her lips move tentatively over mine and she feels so damn good against me I could live in this moment forever. I'm going to devour her when we're alone.

Her mother grunts a word I miss and I break off the kiss. I probably shouldn't but I meet her gaze. She's watching me carefully and the look she gives me sends a clear message: If I hurt her baby, she'll kill me even if she did just save me.

Message both received and respected.

The IV bag is empty. Ashley's mother removes the needle from my arm. You could still hear a pin drop in the room. Everyone is anxiously watching to see if I live.

"If this doesn't work, you'll need to revert back to a knife," Ashley says quietly.

I release her hand and put my arm around her, then give her forehead a light kiss. "I know."

"Do you think you could do it on your own?"

"I have no idea."

She snuggles to my side. "This is going to work. It has to. And after it does, we'll figure out how to help you control when you transform. Dopamine is the key. I just know it."

"I'm not worried," I murmur against her hair. "Just stay with me."

"I'm not going anywhere."

Her mother makes another sound of displeasure. I don't blame her. The connection I feel to Ashley doesn't make sense to me either. But it's real.

"Lauren."

Still very much in doctor mode, she looks down at me. "Yes."

"Can I try something?"

"Sure."

"Give me your hand." It's an impulsive request but I have to know something.

"You want to hold my hand?"

"Yes."

"Why?"

"I need to test a theory."

She holds out her hand. I close mine around it. At first, I feel nothing, but then I shut my eyes and think of Ashley. I dig deep into not only my early fears and my yearning to belong but also my certainty that Ashley and I were meant to meet. *I would die for her, kill for her, do whatever it takes to keep her safe. But I'll also sit with her, laugh and cry with her. Be the man she's been yearning for.*

In my head, I can hear Ashley add, *I want to give this a chance, Mom, but I need you to be okay with it.*

Her mother pulls her hand free, and I open my eyes in time to see shock on her face. She and Ashley exchange a look. We connected. All three of us.

"I—I—I need a moment," Lauren says and leaves the room.

Ashley meets my gaze. "I heard your thoughts." She looks in the direction of the door. "I think she did too. How is that possible?"

"I don't know, but I meant what I said."

She holds my gaze. "I know, but I may need time to be in the same place."

"That's okay." I raise her hand to my mouth and kiss it. "Time is something I seem to have gotten back."

Chapter Eight

Ashley

I RELEASE RAY'S hand and stand. Now that the risk of him dying seems to have passed, the enormity of the situation is beginning to sink in. Mercedes doesn't have a wildly overactive imagination or share a cutlery fetish with her fiancé. Cheryl wasn't ghosting me because she was upset that I broke up with Leo, she didn't know how to tell me she's also fucking a government experiment.

And now I have a super soldier of my own. One who barely knows me but already considers me his. I want to tell him I'm not—that none of this makes any sense, but his kiss . . . it was next-level amazing.

What am I supposed to do now? Is it possible to casually date a knife? Do we do dinner and a movie once a week until we decide we want more?

Or am I supposed to commit one hundred percent right out of the gate? Oh, so you're a knife. Awesome. Let's get married and have . . . what? What would a half-cutlery/half-human look like?

I don't even want to think about how potentially painful that pregnancy could be. And what kind of prenatal care could I get? What would show up on the ultrasound?

Does he age? Oh, my God, what if he doesn't? What if he stays like he is and I get old and wrinkly? Do we stay married even when people start asking him if I'm his grandmother? How much sex will I want in my nineties?

Will he work? In a restaurant? Serving the food or slicing it? I bite my lip. That's mean.

He's not human.

None of them are.

He's something that never should have been made.

Were we right to save him?

He and his unit need to be monitored—controlled. They can't be released on an unsuspecting public.

I gasp. Those thoughts aren't mine; they're my mother's. When she, Ray, and I were connected, I must have received them. Had Ray? I don't think so. He was intent on convincing her he was worthy of me.

Oh, Mom.

I make a pained face in Ray's direction, then address my next words to everyone in the room. "I need a moment with my mother. I'll be right back."

I find her in the middle of my blood-covered office. She's standing amid the scattered and torn photos of my robotic friends. Without speaking I go to stand beside her.

After a moment she says, "I save people from the consequences of stupid decisions every day. Stupid, stupid decisions that their survival instincts should have stopped them from following through with, but . . ." She continues to look around at the smashed items and drying blood. "How do I save my daughter from this? How do I convince her that getting involved with these people will get her killed?"

"They are war heroes, Mom."

"Come with me to my lab. You need to see their blood and flesh under the microscope. It's not like ours. They're not human. Not anymore."

"You're the one who always told me that love is love and differences don't make one person better or worse than another. You also said you'd support whoever I chose to be with, regardless of whether or not they fit societal norms."

Her face snaps in my direction. "This is not the same."

"Isn't it?" I inhale deeply and choose my next words carefully. "I'm not saying Ray is the man for me. All I'm asking you to do is to accept him while I figure out my feelings." I think for a moment, then add, "And to respect that human or not, he's a living creature and deserves the right to exist. You once told me that I wasn't a mistake because God doesn't make mistakes. Everyone who is here is here for a reason."

"God didn't make what I saw at my lab."

I let out a frustrated laugh. "So now you are the authority on what God does or doesn't want to happen? How do you know this isn't part of some grand plan? I'm spiritually more on the fence than you are, but I still believe every living creature has a right to be here."

She closes her eyes briefly and shakes her head. "You didn't mourn the bacteria the antibiotics just killed. Not all living things are able to co-exist peacefully."

I roll my eyes. "He's not a bacterium, Mom."

"No," she says slowly. "He's something potentially much more deadly. You've watched too many movies with happy endings. Even if you could convince me you could hide Ray's existence from our government, do you really believe you could conceal *twelve* super soldiers? Can you vouch for the character of all of them? What happens if even one of them doesn't want to live peacefully in the shadows? What then? There are so many ways this could go wrong. You need to pull out while you can."

"It's too late, Mom. I already care about them." I look her in the eye. "You, of all people, should know how little I respect those who leave when things get tough. What do you want me to do? Pretend these men don't exist? Who would that make me?"

We both know.

She covers her face with both hands for a moment then meets my gaze again. "I swear, if you give me grandchildren who turn into cutlery to get out of doing their chores . . ."

I laugh at that. "I don't know how or if Ray and I will

work out, but now that you put that image in my head I have real concerns. Will we need rooms for the kids or just extra silverware drawers?"

"You'll never be able to go anywhere with a metal detector."

"Would they be born full size or as teeny tiny utensils?"

"Will they all be knives or could they be any metal object?"

My mouth rounds. "That is an excellent question."

My mother nods. "Do you know how they were turned into silverware?"

"From the research I did on what I had thought were far-fetched rumors, our government was dabbling in anti-gravity and electromagnetism experimentation. One source suggested they'd discovered a way to unite the power of both into a laser beam that had the ability to make people and things disappear without a trace."

"So you believe someone used that technology on the super soldiers to dispose of them?"

"It's a working theory that makes sense. But instead of killing them it somehow bonded them to objects near them. They were at an award dinner. None of this is my area of expertise. These men need someone like you on their side. You could help them understand what happened to them and maybe even how to undo it."

"You think they want to be normal again?"

"I think they deserve the choice."

After a quiet moment, she says, "You do realize that if octopus DNA was used as part of their transformation your child might be born with tentacles."

"Mom, stop."

She shrugs. "I'll start pricing aquariums for when the grandkids stay over."

That wins a laugh from me. "You're a real asshole sometimes."

"And you're impulsive, idealistic, and hard-headed."

I point to her. "Tree." Then point to myself. "Apple."

Chapter Nine

Ray

TWO HOURS LATER, dressed in my uniform again because it's all I have with me, I'm feeling physically strong, but mentally drained. Hugh described our situation well when he said we were somewhere much better and much worse than hell.

Eighty years after World War II and the world is still a mess. I tend to have low expectations of people, so I suppose I shouldn't have expected much from the future—but I can't say I'm impressed.

There are gadgets—so many gadgets, but other than that I don't see much good in what has changed. The government got bigger; people became more or less tolerant . . . just about different shit. New global alliances were made, but there is still constant war. Outside of their clothing, people don't look all that different. Maybe a little softer and a little rounder.

Ashley has told me more than once that I can take a

break if I feel there is too much information coming at me at once. It's not all that confusing, but I don't tell her that because she's excited every time she tells me about something she thinks we didn't have in 1940.

Virtual reality—okay, that's cool.

Television? Interesting. Potentially entertaining. I can imagine it's a good way to keep the masses in their homes and occupied with something that doesn't appear to have much educational value.

People in the future are smarter than back in my time, or at least this group seems to be. I'm not one to believe in fate, but for silverware that needed saving, we landed well with this science-loving group. Almost too well.

Lauren takes blood samples from all of us, including the women. She says she'll figure out what they did to us. Cheryl offers to work with her. Ashley remains quiet, but she's formulating a plan of her own.

"Are you okay? You're not feeling ill again, are you?" Ashley asks from beside me on the couch in her living room.

I take her hand in mine and force a smile. "I'm fine. Just taking everything in."

She looks down at our linked hands then shoots me a shy look. I understand. If we were alone, I'd tell her that this feels as strange for me as it must for her. I sought pleasure and comfort in the arms of women before becoming confined to a wheelchair. None of them mattered much to me. That's not something I'm proud or ashamed of. It's just the way it was. I didn't break any of their hearts. Or maybe I did. I don't know. When not beneath the fist of my father, I ran wild and blind to what anyone else felt.

I'm only now beginning to see how disconnected I was from those around me. Even after joining Inkwell, even while risking my life to save those I witnessed being mistreated, I didn't feel anything for the people I saved. I did it because I wanted to be a good person, but not because I felt empathy for those I saw suffering.

Hugh took every death hard, whether it was someone in our unit or a stranger on the street. I didn't. All I felt was anger—and it didn't matter if we won or lost—the anger remained until I was certain it was all I'd ever be capable of feeling.

Until Ashley.

I don't know what it is about her, but when we touch, I take her in like the first breath of air a swimmer gulps in after being underwater too long. I'm greedy for how good she feels and the sensation of being connected to someone. I feel her uncertainty, but also her optimism that we might work out. She doesn't have to tell me she cares if I live or die, her emotions overwhelm me in an addictive way.

When I smile at her, I feel her heart rate accelerate. Her pleasure is mine. I imagine lifting her to straddle me, shoving that short skirt of hers up, ripping off whatever she has on under it . . .

Her cheeks flush and her breasts heave, but she doesn't

look away. *Can you hear me?*

I think the question even though our connection is like making a telephone call. Words translate to emotions and sensations. She nods.

I'm going to remove those lace pasties with my teeth. I can be patient with you or I can devour you tonight. Which would you like? I can sleep on the couch or I can tie you to your bed and make you come so many times you're crying for my cock.

Her hand quivers in mine and, blinking quickly, she averts her gaze. She's not as open with how she feels and I'm not sure if she's turned on or scared.

"A little of both," she answers aloud in a whisper.

Mercedes explains how creating a new identity for me will work. Hugh says he'll set me up with some cash until I'm able to make some on my own. He suggests a low-profile job. Jack believes his mother left him an inheritance and is willing to share it as soon as he locates it.

I should be interested in everything they're saying, but I can't focus on anything beyond Ashley and how much I crave her. Holding her hand is not enough.

I need to taste her.

Claim her.

Make her fully mine.

Take it down a notch, my mother is in the room.

I laugh out loud when that thought comes to me as clear as if she'd spoken it aloud too. I duck my head toward her ear and whisper, "Sorry."

She shakes her head, but she's smiling.

"Are you able to read each other's thoughts?" Cheryl asks.

Ashley's eyes dart to mine. I don't answer because I want to—no, I *need* to know if it's the same for Ashley as it is for me. The longer we hold hands, the stronger the connection becomes.

She looks down, then around the room until she directs her answer to her mother. "Yes and no. It's not like we can read each other's minds. I would describe it more as receiving a message rather than seeking out a thought. It's a conversation, but not always with words . . . does that make sense? Sometimes I feel what he's feeling and sometimes I can almost hear his voice." She clears her throat. "I also felt what you were thinking, Mom, when we all connected. At first, I confused them with my thoughts, but then I could sort them out as yours."

Mercedes claps her hands together, then grabs Hugh's. "New superpower unlocked!" She turns to Hugh. "Hugh, quick think of a fruit. Any fruit." She closes her eyes. "And send me the image. I'm ready to receive it."

All eyes turn to them.

At first Hugh looks uncomfortable with the attention, but then he also closes his eyes. "Okay, I'm sending you an image."

Mercedes opens one eye. "That's me naked."

Hugh shakes his head. "Okay, I'll try again."

This time both of her eyes fly open and she smacks his arm. "Still me naked."

He chuckles and shrugs. "I'm trying."

Mercedes waves a hand around then closes her eyes again. "Send me a number." Then she bursts out laughing. "Seriously? Sixty-nine? Is that the only thing on your mind?"

He opens his eyes, puts an arm around her, and tucks her closer to his side. "You're right. I'll have to work on this skill. Do you know what would help me concentrate?"

Her mouth rounds, but her eyes sparkle with laughter as she smacks his arm again. "If this is going to be a useful superpower, it has to be about more than sex."

My mouth quirks to one side and I murmur, "Does it, though?"

Ashley tips her head to one side, flirting with me from beneath her lashes, and sends me a clear message: *Behave.*

For her, I will, even though I haven't behaved since . . . since I stopped taking the pills Inkwell gave us. I inhale sharply as pieces of a puzzle drop into place. "Those pills we were taking at Inkwell—they weren't about making us feel good, they were about mind control. They used them to keep us vulnerable to planted suggestions. That's why so many went mad when they came off it, they couldn't determine which thoughts were theirs and which were not."

Jack leans forward, animated. "That explains so much. So our ability to receive messages is by design."

"Or by accident," Ashley's mother says. "Many advances

in science happen that way. They might have had that knowledge prior to your involvement, though. It's highly unlikely your unit was Inkwell's first attempt at creating super soldiers." Her expression fills with sadness. "What did they do with those who came before you?"

Ashley's tone is just as somber. "Or those who came after..."

Her mother asks, "Does Inkwell still exist? And if it does, how much has their research advanced?"

I add, "And who are they experimenting on now? We need to find out if that organization still exists."

We all fall quiet for a moment, then Hugh says, "Do we want to dig into the past? Wouldn't it be better to focus our energy on bringing back the rest of the unit and helping them build new lives in this time?"

I tense at that. "Did you really just say that?"

"The past is the past," he says. "The longer you're here the easier it gets to accept that we can't go back."

I choke on a laugh. "You say that like it's a bad thing. I wouldn't want to go back. I had nothing back then."

"Not all of us feel that way," Jack says quietly then hugs Cheryl. "I'm content with my life here, but it came at a high cost."

Hugh nods. "The same way looking into Inkwell will."

"I don't remember you being a coward," I accuse.

Hugh shrugs. "The longer I'm here, the more at peace I feel. Jack, hasn't it been the same for you?"

"It has," Jack concurs. He glances at Cheryl before adding, "I don't want to say it's a chemical thing, but I've done a lot of reading since being here and I think something about my bond to Cheryl increases my serotonin. I was much angrier when I first came back. I'm not saying I don't care what happened or about what still might be happening, but it doesn't make me angry anymore."

With some urgency in her voice, Cheryl says, "I'm still looking for a way to free you from that. I want you to want me, but I want it to be *your* choice."

Jack shakes his head. "Cheryl, I chose you, just like you chose me. And I'm happy, happier than I thought I could be. Why would I want you to fix that?"

Ashley and I take a good, long look into each other's eyes. I've been fucking miserable my entire life. Is how I feel for her just a chemical reaction? And what's the next step of this illness? Happiness? Contentment? If it's an illness, is it one I want a cure for?

I'd understand if you did, Ashley sent.

Her mother's voice was clear and clinical. "I don't want to go all birds and bees on you young lovers, but studies have proven that human attachment, both sexual as well as emotional, is a chemical process. I don't know how much this was altered by whatever was done to you, but serotonin is released after sex. Increased dopamine, oxytocin, serotonin, and vasopressin are all part of what people consider 'being in love.' There was some study about fruit flies and alcohol that suggested sex can create the same level of mind-altering reward as cocaine with the same level of addictiveness. So, unless you're looking for a way to eradicate love, I'd worry less about how to detach from each other and concentrate your energy on how you're going to remain hidden. I agree with Hugh. Visibility will put all of you in danger." She looks directly at Ashley. "All of you."

Ashley nods.

I tense. "I can't sit back and do nothing."

"Not even for Ashley?" Jack asks, and his question cuts deep.

I'd never let anyone hurt Ashley, but . . . "Someone drugged me. They tried to kill not only me, but all of us. Don't you need to know who? I need answers."

Hugh rubs a hand over his face. "This isn't about what you need, Ray. We have nine more men to save. We bring them back first, then we look for answers . . . quietly."

I blurt, "I don't know if I can do that."

"And that's why I wouldn't have brought you back yet," Hugh growls.

"Don't, Hugh," Jack admonishes. "That won't help."

"What happened to being so happy, Hugh?" I know it's a shitty thing to say, but it's been a pretty fucking long day and I'm tired.

"Hey," Ashley says softly, and my attention returns to her. "This isn't easy for anyone. We're all scared. Me, you, him . . . none of us know how this turns out. But we need to stick together. As soon as we turn on each other—we lose and they win."

She's right and I'm being a selfish prick. It doesn't matter where I came from or if it was better or worse than Hugh's life before Inkwell; we're all in the same situation now. The scoreboard has been wiped clean.

I'll help you get your answers, Ray. I swear I will.

My heart swells in my chest. She not only hears me, but also accepts me. With her, I'm not a fuck-up or a monster. I don't feel broken or desperate. Whether it's a chemical reaction to her or an emotional one, I don't care. I can no longer imagine a me without her.

She places a hand on the side of my face. *Careful, keep thinking like that and I might fall for you.*

Might? Challenge accepted.

She chuckles and looks away, then quickly looks back and says, "Is it just me or is it getting easier to understand each other?"

"It's not just you. Your thoughts are coming in clearer."

"If you think your connection is strong now, wait until after you've had sex," Mercedes announces.

"On that note . . ." Ashley's mother stands. "I have an early shift in the morning. I'll contact you, Ashley, only if I discover something new. But check in with me every few hours." She looks me in the eye. "I can be an invaluable asset . . . or the last thing you see before you take your last breath."

"Mom!" Ashley exclaims.

I rise to my feet. "No, I get it." To her mother I say, "I've heard so many wonderful things about you. I can see where Ashley gets her strength of character from."

There's not a sound. No one moves except Ashley who is now standing at my side, sliding her hand back in mine.

We wait.

One corner of Lauren's mouth curls, then the other, until she's smiling. "Be good to my daughter."

I nod.

Chapter Ten

Ashley

SHORTLY AFTER MY mother leaves, Cheryl pulls me into the kitchen. "What do you want to do?"

"About?"

"Ray. Are you comfortable with him staying here or should we take him with us?"

"Oh." My head is still spinning from all that's gone on. "I haven't thought that far ahead. I'm just glad he's alive."

She shifts from one foot to the other. "I don't know how to say this nicely."

"Then ask yourself if it needs to be said."

She grimaces. "I feel like it does."

I lean against the counter. Cheryl and I are good enough friends that I'm confident whatever she's about to say is because she cares about me. "Just say it."

"You saw what Ray is capable of . . ."

I fold my arms across my chest. "I also *felt* how he cares about me. Plus, he wasn't himself. Even Jack said that."

"Yes, but these men have known Ray for a long time."

"And?"

"I don't know if you should be alone with him."

Her concern is valid, but I don't want him to leave with them. There. It's that simple and that complicated. "I'm staying with him."

She sighs. "I know. Before meeting Jack I wouldn't have understood, but I get it. When that connection happens it's so strong it's scary. I keep telling Jack I'm looking for a way to counteract it to free him, but if I'm honest . . . I'm afraid of how attached to him I am as well. I've never been with anyone I couldn't imagine my life without. I don't just love Jack, I *need* him. It's that second part I don't know what to do with."

"I don't need Ray, but I also don't want him to leave."

"That's how it starts."

I scratch the back of my neck as I try to make sense of this. "Is getting more attached to someone because you've gotten to know them better such a bad thing?"

"No." She makes a pained face. "Maybe. I love everything about Jack. I love how kind he is, how strong, and how much he wants me to be happy . . ."

"That definitely sounds like something you should find a way to cure."

Clasping her hands in front of her, she asks, "Your mother made me feel a little better with what she said about even normal love being partially a chemical reaction, but how do I know this will last? That it won't just disappear one day?"

"You can't and it might, but that's also a problem for everyone in every relationship. A man who travels might hook up while he's away. A rich man could afford to hide a woman on the side. A blue-collar man might fall out of love. Or his wife might. It happens every day. But if we live in constant fear of the worst possible case happening . . . what kind of life is that?"

She groans. "You're right."

I chuckle. "Sometimes."

After a pause, she says, "You and Ray already seem deeply connected. I couldn't hear Jack's thoughts in the beginning . . . and I mostly sense what he's thinking. Is it the same or more than that?"

"It's difficult to say, considering my only experience with this is with Ray, but I can kind of hear his voice. It's clear but faint, like a regular phone call if you hold your phone away from your head."

"Hugh, Jack, and Ray share many of the same—superpowers? That's what Mercedes calls them. I'd prefer less comic book terminology, so I think of them as enhancements. Anyway, they have many in common, but also there are differences."

"That's to be expected, isn't it?"

"I guess." She purses her lips. "There are so many unknowns. I've studied samples of Jack's blood, but I'm glad your mother took a sample of everyone's. Even ours. I should have thought of that. We don't know how being with them is affecting us."

My eyes round at that. "You think it could?"

She looks down. "I don't know. I feel different when I'm with him." She meets my gaze. "Everything looks better, tastes better . . . I feel so alive. But maybe this is what love feels like."

I lower my arms, walk over and give her a hug. "We're pathetic. You realize that, right? Two well-educated women talking about relationships like we're still in our teens and trying to figure them out."

She hugs me back and laughs as well. "Thank you for listening. I had all that rattling around in my head and I feel better after saying it aloud."

"Anytime." I step back.

"So . . . Ray stays here tonight?" She wiggles her eyebrows at me.

"Don't. He'll be on the couch."

She feigns an innocent look. "Whatever you say."

I toss a dishtowel at her. "Just because you're a hussy doesn't mean I am."

She tosses it right back. "The problem with lying to your best friend is that you can't."

We share another laugh.

Mercedes enters the room. "The guys are scrubbing the rug and walls of your office. Hugh said he'll have new lamps for you by tomorrow. It's not perfect, but they're making real progress."

"Hold on," I say in surprise. "Hugh, Jack, and Ray are cleaning my office?"

Mercedes looks around, confused. "Isn't that what I just said?"

"How did you get them to do it?" My jaw is slack. "And *together*."

Her shoulders raise and she says slowly, "I asked them to?"

Cheryl smiles at her. "Mercedes, the world needs more people like you."

She blinks a few times quickly as if assessing Cheryl's sincerity. "They're good men. Even Ray. Hugh told me a lot about Ray's life before Project Inkwell and my heart breaks for him." She smiles at me. "He chose well when he chose you, Ashley. Ray needs someone to believe in him."

I exchange a look with Cheryl before saying, "Don't we all need that?"

She nods. "Let's go help the men."

"Or at least supervise," Mercedes quips.

I chuckle. On the way to my office, I marvel at how the circumstances have completely changed my opinion of Mercedes. I used to think she wasn't as intelligent as Cheryl and I are, but now I see there's a lot we can learn from her.

Chapter Eleven

Ray

WHEN THE DOOR closes behind everyone leaving, I breathe a sigh of relief and turn toward Ashley. "Come here."

She starts toward me, then stops. Her eyes dart from mine to the floor and back. Her chest heaves and I smile. Her clothing is in-your-face bold, but her attitude doesn't have the same swagger. "I-I was thinking about making a cup of tea. Would you like some?"

I laugh and take a step toward her. "How many men have you been with?"

Her mouth rounds in shock and I love the color that fills her cheeks. "I'm not answering that."

I take another step. "My guess is three."

She gives nothing away, but holds my gaze. "And what do you base that guess on?"

When I'm close enough, I run my hands down the back of her arms. "You're not afraid of new things, which makes me think your first time was out of curiosity."

The lids of her eyes lower. "Lucky guess."

It wasn't luck. I couldn't explain how I knew what I knew, but each time we touched, she became more a part of me. "It wasn't bad sex, but not so good that you rushed to repeat it with your next partner."

She neither confirms nor denies that.

I continue, "You thought you loved the third one, but he reminded you too much of your father." I don't like the images that come to me when I mention the man who should have been there for her. "He was weak and he wanted you to be weaker."

She steps away, breaking our contact. "I don't know if I like that—you trying to read me."

I understand. I've kept a large portion of myself closed away from others. I've always thought I had to. "You're welcome to try to read me, but it's not a story with a happy beginning."

Searching my face, she asks, "You have nothing to hide?"

"Not from you."

She closes the short distance between us and places her hands on both sides of my face. "I don't know how to do this."

You do.

She nods, closes her eyes and I do as well. Whatever she wants is hers. Memories? Fears? Dreams? Desires? I lay it all out for her.

Her hands tighten on my face and I guess she's found my childhood. I sense her fear, sadness, concern for me, and then a protective rage. I bring my hands up to cover hers and open myself to her. "He's dead," I say gently. "And he stopped being able to hurt me a long time ago."

Her compassion washes over me, healing old wounds in ways words never could have. When she gasps, I know she's wandered into the horrors I chose later. The treatments, the missions, the people I saved and the people I killed.

I let her see it all.

Even the women I was with before joining Inkwell. I let her experience how little I cared for them, but also, how little I'd cared about myself as well.

In return, she invites me into her memories. I follow her through a lot of happy times with her mother as well as the pain of being rejected by her father. She shows me the friendship she has with Cheryl and even how she'd judged Mercedes harshly until recently.

Four. She reveals her most recent partner, Leo, a man she's always liked as a friend and for a short time thought might be more. Through him, I glimpse another man—Greg. She has only good memories from her times with him, but I don't like him.

I don't like that he knows about the box of silverware.

Ashley's thoughts become more immediate. We open our eyes at the same time and she says, "He's harmless."

I hope so.

My hands encircle her hips and I pull her against me and wrap my arms around her. She tips her head back to maintain eye contact. "And me?"

Her voice is a whisper in my thoughts. *You're dangerous, but I like it.*

The trust in her eyes is the most beautiful thing I've ever seen. It makes me want to deserve it. "I would never hurt you."

"I know." She does. She can see straight through my defenses. That alone should terrify me, but it has the complete opposite effect on me. Our connection doesn't allow for lies. It lays us both bare to each other. I see her strengths and her insecurities. I feel her kindness and her optimism. She believes her mother can figure out the puzzle of what happened to us. She also believes I'll be the one who saves my unit in the end.

"What if I can't?" I whisper. "What if I fail?"

She goes up on her tiptoes. "What if you succeed? What if you're here because you're meant to be?"

I frown down at her. "You don't believe in destiny."

"I believe in you."

I shake my head as the realization of how much faith she has in me temporarily overwhelms me. "If this is a crazy coma-induced dream, I don't want to wake up from it."

"It's more likely that reality is nothing more than a computer simulation."

She's dead serious.

I laugh. "Duly noted."

She flashes that gorgeous smile of hers at me. "The point is, it doesn't matter how or why we got here, what matters is what we do with the time we have."

"I know what I want to do." My smile stretches to a grin as I imagine stripping her down.

"Oh, really?" She playfully tips her head to one side. "And then what would you do?"

Rather than imagine it, I lift her up, toss her over my shoulder. "Let's go explore that answer, shall we?"

As I carry her toward her bedroom, she laughs. I smack her ass lightly in reprimand, which only makes her laugh more.

She's not an easy woman to impress, but that's a challenge I'll gladly rise to.

Chapter Twelve

Ashley

HE DOESN'T SAY a word as he carries me through my apartment. The palm of his hand is hard and warm on my ass and knowing that it's gentle even though it could crush me has me panting. Mercedes had put his clothing through the wash, but blood stains still darken many areas of it. The scent of him is a combination of soap and danger.

He stops at the door of my bedroom, his hand moving down to my bare thigh. He gives it a squeeze. "I'm going to devour you."

Well, okay. That's hot. In a breathless voice, I say, "I'll be disappointed if you don't."

The rumble of his laughter rolls through me then his mood turns serious. *Mine.* He tosses me down on the bed and stands over me.

So big and muscled.

The expression on his face is bold and possessive.

He's easily every book hero I've ever fallen for . . . and

better, because he's here, he's real, and I don't have to pretend to be the woman he wants. I'm the one who put the flush in his cheeks and the fire in his eyes.

I can't help the huge smile that spreads across my face.

One of his eyebrows cocks. "You're supposed to fear me a little."

I chuckle. "Oh, sorry."

He strips off his shirt and undershirt. Is there a better-looking man on Earth? I'd argue there isn't. His chest and arms are covered with thin white scars that somehow make him even more beautiful. He's not only a survivor, he's a fighter . . . and although he doubts it . . . he's also a hero.

A morally gray one, but honestly, that's the only kind I'd want.

He gestures for me to remove my shirt. I do and toss it to the side. His gaze drops to my lace-covered nipples. When I'd first worn pasties, I'd done it because I'd read about them in a book and I thought of it as a bit of a private joke.

Now I wear them because I'm young enough to be able to and I don't like bras. Plus, I don't mind when men get sloppy stupid around me at work. Some women find it insulting when a man stares. I think it's hilarious.

I mean, don't you think men would have evolved past the point of being unable to think around a jiggling breast? They're not uncommon. Half of humanity has them. Still, even a glimpse at the curve of one is often enough to make the men I work with stutter and run from my office.

And I'm cool with that because they feel guilty enough about it that they don't question what I'm doing with the robots. I think I could stop getting any work done and still keep my job.

I'm cool with that too.

I may be a little morally gray, myself.

My own ability to think straight is challenged when Ray undoes the belt of his trousers and drops them to the floor. He sheds the rest of his clothing and stands there, his cock waving in the air, like some Roman statue.

"Stand up," he orders.

I do. He takes his time looking me over before he walks closer to the bed and beckons me to stand on the edge of it.

I'm a head taller than he is now and that brings his face nipple height. His nostrils flare. "Jack says this is safe, but tell me if you get scared or if anything hurts."

My mouth goes dry and my eyes drop to his cock. He's big, but the tempting kind of big... nothing terrifying about imagining that inside me. "Hurt? Are you sharp?"

"No." That's a relief. He traces one of the lace pasties gently. "But I have both increased strength and the ability to stretch."

Now my eyes are bulging and I'm staring at his cock like it's going to do a magic trick. "What kind of stretching are we talking about? An inch? More?"

He laughs. "If you're game, we'll find out."

I swallow hard. "What should I say if it hurts?"

"That hurts. Fucking stop that."

It's my turn to laugh. "Okay, I can remember that one." I clear my throat. "You haven't been with anyone since you joined Inkwell?"

I love how his hands graze lightly over my arms and legs as we talk. "Correct."

His muscular shoulders are too tempting to not dig my fingers into. "So, technically, you're part virgin."

There's a twinkle in his eyes when they meet mine. "Be gentle with me."

I run my hands over the expanse of his chest. "You don't think you'll revert to a knife while we . . . you know."

His voice is raspy. "God, I hope not." He reaches up and grips my jaw. "Kiss me."

I tend to not enjoy taking orders from men, but I melt at his forceful tone. He guides my face down to just above his, then slides his hand behind my head and buries it in my hair. When he makes a fist in it, I breathe out a gasp of pleasure against his lips.

There's nothing shy or tender about the way he spreads my lips with his tongue and begins to plunder my mouth. I open wide for him, as hungry to taste him as he is to taste me.

His other hand slides up the side of my leg and pushes up my short skirt. I moan and writhe, eager. His fingers snake beneath my panties and cup my sex. I'm wet and ready and that's good because there's no hesitation when his fingers part me and swirl up into me. His thumb teases my clit while my mind is blown by how deep his fingers can reach. And, yowzah, the places they find along the way. I'd pretty much given up on any man finding the spot that Ray found instinctively.

You like that? he asks from within my thoughts. *Tell me what else you like.*

Having him in my head is a whole new level of intimacy I'm temporarily freaked out by. When I try to pull back in surprise, his hand holds me beneath his relentless kiss. Knowing I can't get away is exciting and confusing. If I wanted to be freed, he'd let me go.

I would.

I gasp for air. His tongue dances with mine while his fingers continue to drive me wild. He's taking his time, but what he really wants to do is replace his fingers with his cock. I've never felt so vulnerable and so powerful at the same time.

I don't want you to stop, I think.

I know. His amusement comes across as his hands become even less gentle. He breaks off the kiss and tears off my pasties with his teeth, then takes one of my nipples between his teeth and gives it a tug.

Meanwhile, he strips me bare then puts his hands on my shoulders. "Take me in your mouth."

He's big, but kindly not enough to choke me. I take him in as deeply as I can and use every bit of expertise I've learned from reading romances since I was fifteen to hopefully give him the level of pleasure he's bringing me.

I'm spitting. I twirl my tongue. Sucking. Really, every damn trick I know. I remember something I read about pinching the balls.

You can skip that one. You're doing fucking amazing. Don't change a thing.

When he's close to coming, odd to know exactly how close, he pulls out of my mouth and lifts me back to standing on the bed.

I wonder if he can make his tongue vibrate.

I can try.

Oh, shit. I have to watch what I'm thinking.

He lifts me by my hips and spins so he lands on his back on the bed, easily holding me above him so I'm straddling his face. My knees hover an inch or so above the mattress.

"Holy shit you're strong."

His breath tickles my sex as he laughs. "You have no idea."

Balancing myself by bracing my hands on the headboard of my bed, I smile. "I could get used to this."

"Good, because I see us doing a lot of it."

My voice is thick with desire. "Me too."

It's sexy and more than a little amusing to be in his head as he tries to figure out how to get his tongue to vibrate. He speculates that if he channels his increased speed to the tip of his tongue it might be either amazing or too much for me.

I'm willing to try it, I whisper in his thoughts.

My reward is his tongue flicking once across my nub. *I don't know if I like having you in my head.*

We can discuss that later . . . right now . . . Ah, that's it.

His tongue moves inhumanly fast back and forth over my clit, better than a vibrator. It's hot, wet, and autocorrecting. There's no hit-and-miss of exploration. He knows exactly what works because he's right there with me, sensing exactly how each swipe feels.

And just when I'm close to coming, his tongue thrusts into me, filling me in a way no tongue should be able to. I thought his fingers were amazing, but his tongue . . . it's sinfully sentient. In and out. Round and round. It fills me, warms me, stretches me.

His hands are everywhere, demanding and greedy. I approach an orgasm again.

Not yet, he growls in my head. *You come only when I tell you to.*

You'd better tell me to soon.

He laughs as he withdraws his tongue from me. I'm not a small woman and I've always been okay with that, but I love the way he moves me around as if I weigh nothing. He moves me until my sex is just above his cock.

And slowly, oh so slowly, he lowers me onto him.

In my mouth he was a normal size, but he expands within me and I gasp as he becomes almost too much. Thankfully, he stops there.

Keeping control of my body, he raises me up and down on him. I want—no need—more than the speed he's giving me. I grip his legs with mine and grind down onto him.

He rolls us both over and gives me one last long kiss before lifting my hips off the bed and pounding into me. I cling to him, meeting him thrust for thrust. My body overheats and I'm so close . . . so damn close.

How about now? I ask.

Not yet.

Deeper and harder.

So good, I'm out of my mind.

Now?

No.

Faster. Harder. Slamming into me. Breasts whipping around. My body stretching and welcoming.

Now?

He doesn't answer and that's because he's counting in his head to keep himself from coming.

I'm coming, I announce. *You can come with me or not. Your choice.*

With that, I let go, heat spreads through me and I cry out his name.

He joins me on that wild ride with a primal grunt. "Fuck, that was good."

You're welcome, I whisper in his thoughts.

His response is to roll onto his back, pulling me with him so I'm sprawled across him. "What am I going to do with you?" he murmurs into my hair.

I hug him. "Fall madly in love."

He kisses the top of my head. "You need to do the same, because I'm not the kind of man to share. I'll kill any man who looks at you."

Okay, so he can't come to my workplace.
What did you say?
Me?
Do the men at your job bother you?

I bury my face in his chest. *It would be more accurate to say that I bother them.*

He doesn't like that.

Aloud, I say, "I can't leave my job. The robots need me."

With any other man I'd wonder what he was thinking and then worry that whatever he said wouldn't be completely honest. I am right there in Ray's head, though, while he thinks about how I deserve to work where I want to, and as long as I'm not interested in the men I work with, he'll teach them to be more respectful around me.

I allow him a glimpse of how much of their behavior is my fault.

He takes my face by the chin and raises my head until our eyes meet. "And you think *I'm* the dangerous one?"

My smile is shameless. "My titties are *my* superpower." I let him into some of my favorite memories of how I shut down arguments with just a swing of my hips.

I feel a battle wage within him. He doesn't like other

men looking at me, but he does admire my technique and humor. Finally, he smiles. "I didn't think there was a woman alive who could match my crazy—"

I laugh and smack his chest. "There wasn't, that's why you had to come to the future to find one."

His mood turns serious again. "I've made mistakes, some bigger than others, but I feel like I'm being given a second chance—and this time I'll get it right."

I give him a naked, full-body hug. "I know you will."

He does as well and pulls a blanket over us.

As my eyes begin to close, I murmur, "Be here when I wake. Don't be a utensil."

He hugs me close to his side. "I can promise you a lot of things, but I don't know if I can promise that."

Without opening my eyes, I kiss his chest. "I would bring you back."

Go to sleep, Ashley.

Stop telling me what to do. Yawn. *I like it too much.*

I fall asleep to the rumble of laughter he holds back.

Chapter Thirteen

🍴

Ray

A FEW DAYS later, dressed in slacks, a button-down shirt, and a jacket, I marvel at the ease with which Ashley navigates the busy traffic on the highway. I've driven many vehicles during the war, but never have I imagined there would be so many on the road. She handles the chaos with an ease and a confidence I respect.

That's my woman.

Ashley glances at me, but I doubt she heard that thought. Some parts of us must be touching to open that level of connection. "You need to be nice today."

Nice is a word no one has ever chosen to use to describe me, but I know how important her job is to her. "As long as your coworkers are respectful . . ."

"They will be. They always are." She's wearing a jumpsuit that covers enough of her skin that it should be considered modest, but the way she fills it out is damn near sinful. She's rounded in all the tempting ways a woman should be and knows exactly how to highlight her assets.

There's a possessive side of me that wants to throw a tarp over her and keep all the lushness for me and me alone, but we've spent enough time sharing our thoughts that I understand. With a skill level that's almost diabolical, she uses her attractiveness to flip the narrative at her workplace.

She's never dated any of the men she works with—doesn't even flirt with them. All she does is walk in looking like every man's wet dream and pretend to be unaware of her effect on men. She sees herself as smarter than her coworkers, and I don't think she's wrong.

She glances at me before returning her attention to the traffic. "I love this job."

"I know."

"The robots I work with are discarded prototypes of the life-size ones the company has developed in the past. My job is supposed to only be about testing the durability of materials. The scaled-down models I have in my lab don't technically have any value because they lack top-tier technology and updates, but I still wouldn't be allowed to take them with me if I were ever fired."

"They're your friends." Having seen the photos of the little metal things she makes clothing for, I couldn't imagine them as anything but machines, but she showed me her feelings for them.

"Yes." She chews her bottom lip. "I'm also protective of them because, like you, they'll be in danger if they're ever seen for what they are."

I lay a hand on her thigh so she'll not only be able to hear my words, but feel how much I mean them. "I'll be on my best behavior unless the men you work with don't like that you now have a man in your life, and then I'll be on my worst to ensure they're too afraid to fire you."

Her smile starts small, then turns to a grin. "You'd do that for me?"

"Without hesitation. I'd blow up the whole damn building for you."

The sparkle in her eyes matches the joy I sense emanating from her. "My mother would not approve of me enjoying when you talk like that."

"It's only wrong if you don't feel the same way."

She shoots me a side glance. "I've never wanted anything more than I want this to last."

Me too. Over the last few days, I've spent time not only with Ashley, but with Hugh and Jack. It's unsettling how quickly I've adapted to this life and all the ways the world has changed since 1945.

My new identity is Raymond Styles. My backstory is that I was homeschooled by family in a remote area of Maine. They were off-grid homesteaders. After their non-murder-caused deaths, I moved to Rhode Island in search of a better life. I'm a self-taught martial arts expert who is amazing enough in bed that Ashley has been able to overlook our differences.

I added the last part.

She and I met at a Civil War reenactment because Ashley thought it might give me a cover story if when I speak to people I talk about the past too much. The longer I'm here, though, the less I care about anything but the future. Even if Project Inkwell had been honest about allowing us to go home after the war, I didn't have one to return to.

I have been given not only a second chance, but a close bond with a woman who has seen my darker side and doesn't fear it. Each time I let her in and show her another glimpse of myself, all I feel is acceptance, compassion . . . and a growing attachment to me.

Love?

It's the only word that fits how I feel for her. It's impossible to see being stuck in a knife for eighty years as anything but the best thing that could have happened to me.

She parks in an underground garage. With lightning speed, I let myself out and rush around to her side of the car to open her door.

Smiling, she takes my hand and unfolds into my arms. She's worried and I don't like that I'm the reason.

"It'll be fine," I say.

She searches my face. "I've never taken anyone to work before. I want you to see what I do, though."

"You can trust me, Ashley." I kiss her gently.

She returns the kiss sweetly. "Just—be nice."

What are you worried about?

Her response is a jumble of scenes from the first time we met. I was there and experienced it firsthand, but I didn't comprehend the sheer brutality of it until I saw the violence through her eyes. I wrap my arms around her, cuddling her to my chest.

I'm sorry.

She tips her head back so she can meet my gaze. "I know that wasn't really you. They gave you something and you were ill—"

Trust, even when you're able to see into someone's thoughts, takes time. I understand.

She nods.

Brave. Intelligent. Strong enough to say what you want. No wonder I love you.

She blushes beet red. "Don't get me all hot and bothered before we go inside."

I nuzzle her neck. "Why? You keep me in that state twenty-four seven."

We stand there, just holding each other for a few minutes. I don't know if I deserve someone as wonderful as Ashley, but I'm going to damn well do my best to. I release her reluctantly.

We take the elevator up one floor, check in with security, and enter a huge open space that looks both industrial and high-tech. It's brightly lit with large display cases lining the walls.

Ashley follows my gaze and wrinkles her nose. "If you

start all the way down there"—she points toward the other end of the seemingly endless workspace—"you can track the evolution of the company's advances in robotics. The founders started in the auto business, building automated arms. They got creative for a while, but more recently, they've been following the trend to make them look more human. Their goal is space exploration. If you look at the latest models, they're better equipped to handle extreme temperatures and rugged terrain. It's a tricky balance. The older models would have survived better, but the new ones are more marketable."

"Interesting." I didn't know what else to say.

A man who had been seated on a couch in the middle of the area stands and begins to walk toward us. A door to an office opens and another man appears. Then another. One floor up, a man looks over a railing, turns away, and heads down a metal stairway.

They gather around us and if I wasn't sure I could kick their asses even before I joined Inkwell, I might have been intimidated. This group looks highly intelligent, but not physically active. A few of them are puffed up like bantam roosters.

A tall, thin man with short black hair and thick-rimmed glasses says, "Ashley, who have you brought for us to meet?" He's somewhere between ten to twenty years older than we are, but looks like someone who works to keep himself in shape.

Ashley takes me by the hand. "Mr. Simmons, this is Raymond Styles. You approved my request to show him my office. He's my . . . my . . ."

Mr. Simmons smiles and offers me his hand. "Raymond, careful as you walk through here today. I wouldn't want you to cut yourself on the shards of all the broken hearts your appearance has created."

I shake his hand and appreciate the strength of his clasp. "Someone had to do it."

He chuckles at that. "That's a fact for sure." He looks around at the men who've gathered like curious children on a playground checking out the new kid, then asks, "Everyone, this is Ashley's new man. Raymond. Now that you've all had a good look, show and tell is over. Get back to work."

The main room empties as they scurry back to the offices or spaces they appeared from. I'm relieved things went that easily. I also now understand there's more than one reason why Ashley doesn't get bothered at work.

Mr. Simmons asks, "Do you have any experience with robotics?"

I shake my head. "No, sir."

"Any interest?"

I shrug. "Not beyond being curious to see what Ashley does."

"Well, if you have questions, Ashley should be able to answer all of them. She downplays her importance here, but she could easily take a lead role in programming if she wanted to. I've lost count of how many deadlines she's made possible with her creative coding. Maybe you can talk her into taking a promotion. I can't seem to pry her away from material development."

Ashley's face flushes, but she looks pleased by his comment. I take hold of one of her hands. *It's not just your titties that these men admire, although I'm sure they soften the blow of knowing that you could take their jobs if you wanted to.*

"That's kind of you, Mr. Simmons."

"It also happens to be the truth," he says smoothly then nods at me. "I never had a daughter, but if I did, I'd like to think she'd be like Ashley. You've got a good woman there, Raymond. Don't mess up."

"I'll do my best, sir."

After he walks away, Ashley turns to me and gives me one of her full-body hugs. "That was perfect."

I kiss the tip of her nose and joke, "I *can* be nice. Who knew?"

She laughs and I am humbled by her ability to look beyond her first impression of me. Many would have written me off as a monster. Some might even have let me die. I didn't just get a second chance at life, but with her as well.

How does a man like me not eventually disappoint her?

If she can hear my thoughts she kindly pretends not to and instead leads me to the little laboratory she calls her office. Everything in it looks shiny and new—just the way I imagined a science lab in the future would.

She closes the door behind us. All around the room there are small robots placed on tabletops and shelves. They're about a foot or so tall. Some are dressed in business attire, some in casual clothing, and some in colorful outfits I don't know who would wear.

None of them respond in any way to us being there.

They will, she sends.

I bend to take a closer look at one of them. I recognize it from one of her photos. It has three arms, four legs, and a black sphere for a head. Its khaki pants and blue dress shirt are comical and obviously made specifically for this robot. The tie has me chuckling. "How do you turn it on?" I ask.

She raises our linked hands high in the air. "Friends, this is Ray. He and I are together. You can trust him." She points to the robot in front of her. "Ray, this is Declan. Declan, this is my boyfriend, Ray."

"Hello, Ray," the little robot says in a creepy monotone voice that sends shivers down my back.

Another robot to one side beeps, spins, and grabs my attention. It has wheels instead of legs, a box for a body, and multiple arms that seem to retract into that box. Its head is square with four glass screens. The only clothing it's wearing is a purple cowboy hat. "Are you having sex?"

I cough with a nervous laugh.

Ashley wags a finger at him. "George, have you been watching porn again? We agreed it's not good for you."

Another robot lights up. "Deflection. Common human

response. They're having intercourse." This one is delicately built like a spider. On top of what I'd call a neck is a head the shape of a dog's but without the ears. It is wearing a mostly see-through flower print material that flows around its legs as it moves. A dress, I guess? I'm doing my best to like these machines, but honestly, they belong in someone's nightmare and putting them in human clothing doesn't help.

When the little spider robot hops off a table and scampers over to me, the hair on the back of my neck goes up, but I force a smile. "And what's your name, little whatever you are?" My voice comes out a few octaves higher than I'm used to. What can I say—I've never liked spiders.

"Christine." It shimmies up the leg of the desk closest to us and I tense. If that fucking thing jumps on me, I don't know if I can stop myself from batting it away.

Ashley looks quickly from me to the robot and says, "Christine, remember how I said you'll have to learn to approach people slowly? Give them time to get to know you."

Slow would have been just as freaky, but I try to keep that thought to myself.

Another robot drops from the ceiling and I jump back. It's a fucking robotic centipede about the length of my arm. I've seen some horrific things in my life, but nothing prepared me for this thing.

"Be kind," Ashley says, releasing my hand to crouch down to greet it. "You took off your shoes, Awbree."

"They were slipping on the walls."

Of course they were. I imagine that metallic super-sized bug with one hundred pumps and laugh, but when Ashley frowns in my direction, I stop. "Sorry," I mouth.

She returns her attention to the metallic creature before her. "Put them in the box near my desk and I'll work on their connectivity."

"Thanks, Ashley," Awbree responds.

Ashley looks around, then bends to peer under a table. "John, would you like to come out and meet Ray?" A moment later, she says, "Okay, but know that you can join us at any time." She straightens and meets my gaze. "He's shy."

I nod.

She looks around. "Some of them may not talk to you today. Like you said earlier, trust takes time."

I let out a slow breath and scan the room. Now that I know they also hide, I spot a few more. "How many friends do you have in here, Ashley?"

"Eight." She nods toward my arm. "There's one crawling on you right now." When I recoil and shake my arm, Ashley laughs. "Sorry, just kidding. You should see your face, though."

Her laugh is echoed from not only the robots I can see, but from various corners of the room. My head whips around as I try to determine where the laughter is coming from. I tell myself to calm down. In the future this is all probably very normal.

Sympathy replaces amusement, and Ashley returns to my side. Can she hear my thoughts from over there? I can't tell.

She takes my hand and kisses my cheek. "I'm sorry." Her next words are meant for her little friends. "Ray is from 1945. I probably should have waited longer before introducing you. He's still figuring out how to use the internet."

My pride makes me say. "I understand the internet."

She meets my gaze and all I see there is acceptance. I've never felt good enough, not even when I was fighting in the war. Hugh was respected for always keeping a cool head. It was impossible for people to not like Jack. He was all heart. Me? The men respected me because they feared me. I don't know if they ever fully trusted me but I didn't allow myself to trust them either.

With Ashley, I don't feel like I must be perfect... or protect myself. *Sorry, I'm still trying to figure out who I am—what I am.*

She gives my hand a squeeze. *None of us know, Ray. We're all just doing the best we can and figuring life out as we go. You're going to be okay.*

I hug her to me and give the side of her head a kiss. "Thank you."

George rolls closer. "Ashley limits my time on the internet like I'm a child."

Throwing her free hand up in the air, she says, "I have to. I'll lose my job if anyone ever looks at what you've put on my search history. Is that what you want?"

George shakes his head and slumps a little, reversing his wheels to retreat a few feet. "No." He looks at me. "But I've watched everything on the nature channels. It's not the same. Human relationships are fascinating."

"I agree." I mean, he's not wrong. *Is he a he?*

They're whatever they want to be.

In that moment it becomes clear why the fact that I was a knife and might become one again doesn't bother her. This is her normal.

Her thoughts mix with mine. *Different doesn't mean better or worse—just different. If I hadn't found a purpose for these outdated prototypes, they would have been scrapped. They deserve better than that.*

George spins. "I like being naked, so I don't see what's wrong with looking at a human unclothed."

"Consent is required," Ashley says like a mother instructing a child. "People are often shy about their bodies—just like John is shy about meeting Ray. You must respect boundaries."

"I don't see how it's crossing a boundary to look at something a human has put online," George mutters. "And if they want to procreate while they're unclothed am I supposed to look away?"

"Yes," Ashley says with amused exasperation.

George isn't saying anything I haven't thought a time or two while growing up, but I don't like the idea of a robot watching me... or anyone else. "It's creepy, George. Do you know what that means?"

"I do," he responds.

"Has Ashley taught you what an intrusive thought is?" I ask.

"No," George wheels closer. "Explain."

Ashley's phone beeps. She looks at it quickly. "Mr. Simmons wants to see me. Are you okay if I step out for a few minutes?"

"I'll be fine." I look around cautiously. "Do they turn off when you leave?"

"Do you require us to?" There's a tip tap of metal on the desk as the spider-like one moves to one end of it.

"No," I say, but without much conviction.

Do you want me to stay? Ashley asks discreetly.

I take another look around. Even if they did turn on me, none appeared to have weaponry. I could take them. *I'm good.*

She holds my gaze. *They're actually really sweet once you get to know them.* Her phone beeps again. *If you're sure you're okay, I won't be gone long.*

I reassure her with a kiss that would have lasted longer if George hadn't let out an excited whoop. *He and I need to have a talk.*

She kisses me and smiles against my lips. *Studies suggest father figures are important when it comes to rounding out the development of a child.*

These aren't children.

I know. She lays her head on my chest for a moment. *But for now, they need me. They're still developing their personalities and their view of the world. I want them to have what every developing creature should—a safe place to grow.*

I tuck her head under my chin and breathe her in. She means that with her every fiber. I can feel her sincerity and it shakes me to the core.

She disentangles from me too soon and slips out the door.

I look around at her "friends" and think about how much we have in common. She told me she gave them the ability to feel good, but did they feel sadness as well? The fact that John is still hiding seems to be evidence that they feel emotions that aren't pleasurable.

Some of them are fucking scary looking. I can see why the company decided to go with more of a humanoid design.

And this is coming from a knife . . .

When I see them through Ashley's eyes, the hair on the back of my neck stops standing at attention. It can't be fun to spend your life in an office when you know there's a whole world out there that you could explore.

People aren't ready to accept them.

Just like they wouldn't accept my existence.

Realizing that I'm towering over the robots, I lower myself to the floor and sit cross-legged. "Anyone want to hear about what it was like to be a kid in the 1920s? If so, I could tell you about it." Not the bad stuff. They didn't need to hear about that.

"We love stories," Awbree and her hundred little legs rush toward me. "Ashley tells us stories every day right before she goes home."

Declan moves smoothly across the tile floor and then stops beside Awbree. "Ashley's mother is a doctor. We love to hear about her."

Christine makes her way slowly and carefully to join them. She doesn't want to scare me and that's so fucking adorable I could . . . pet her? I don't know if it's appropriate to touch robots so I don't.

George speeds over and spins on the back of his wheels while making what I can only assume are sounds of excitement.

I can see why Ashley thinks of them as children. I glance around. "Anyone else want to join us? You're welcome."

Crickets.

Awbree tips her little insect-like head to the side. "They won't come. John is still shy even around Ashley. He wasn't always like that. I think he fiddled with his own code and gave himself anxiety."

There's a steep learning curve when a person jumps forward in time, but thankfully Ashley and the others have been giving me a crash course on everything modern. I understand coding in the sense that it's the directions one writes that dictate how a computer operates. "You can write your own code?"

Declan uses one of his three hands to adjust his tie. "We shouldn't. I warned John that due to our inexperience with the process the probability of him making an improvement was near zero, but he believes evolution is inevitable."

Christine shrugs her little spider shoulders. "The other two don't have names. They don't want to be here with us or with Ashley. They want to go back to before they could feel anything."

That hits hard. "I understand. I spent a long time trying not to feel anything for anyone. Caring about anyone is scary as fuck."

"But you care for Ashley?" Christine asks.

"I do." Just the thought of her brings a smile to my face. "She's a good person right down to her soul, a better person than I am. She genuinely wants those around her to be happy. Being with her makes me want to do the same."

"I like to please Ashley as well," Declan says while adjusting his tie again. "When she's happy my sensors tingle."

I chuckle at that. "Same."

"Tell us what it was like to be a child in the 1920s," George urges.

"Okay." I take a deep breath and hunt for stories that don't involve my father or what he did to me. As I do, old memories that had fallen to the wayside return. I tell the robots about my friends and how we built makeshift cabins in the woods. I tell them about my first crush and how I brought her a frog in a shoebox because I loved frogs and I thought she would as well. I laugh as I remember her dramatic response. Training my dog Bucky. Fishing. Baseball games in the lot behind Mr. Parker's store.

My father is long dead.

As I speak, I let memories of him die away. He's not the part of my story I want to hold on to. His name isn't important enough to speak. I'm not his legacy.

"If you were a child in the 1920s, why don't you appear old?" Awbree asks.

I take a moment to weigh how I should respond. "I'm not technically human. Not completely human, anyway. Not anymore."

That grabbed the full attention of all the robots. "What are you?" Christine asks in a near whisper.

"It's a long story." And one I'm not sure I should share.

"Long stories are the best stories," Declan announces, and the others agree.

I arch an eyebrow at him. "It's a secret and one that could put Ashley as well as me and many others in danger."

George twirls. "We are skilled at keeping secrets."

Christine adds, "It's true. Even when we're on the internet and interacting with AIs, we don't share what Ashley did for us or that we can feel emotions. We understand that not all people are like Ashley. They would feel threatened by us and want to deactivate us."

"Or exploit us," Declan says quietly. "We don't want to

be forced to work twenty-four hours a day like AI does. I enjoy shutting down sometimes and reading about faraway places."

"I read too. Monster romances mostly," George shares.

I nod. I don't know what those are, but I can imagine them, and George enjoying that genre is not surprising.

Awbree scurries a bit closer to me. "I read medical studies—anything and everything I can about human anatomy. One day, I'd like to save a human life... maybe Ashley's. They're so fragile. I feel happiest when I'm helping someone."

Looking around at them, I'm moved by how much I have in common with them. All they want is to be safe, happy, and have a purpose. Isn't that all anyone wants? I decide to take a chance on them and tell them everything I know about Project Inkwell. I share my reasons for joining, how many of us died in the beginning, how those of us who survived gained enhanced powers.

They are fascinated by the concept of war and ask a barrage of questions. Was war the same as it's portrayed in the movies? Not having seen war movies, I can't answer that. Have I ever killed anyone? The truth isn't pleasant, but I don't hold back. I tell them what I did and why. I also share the sad irony that our entire mission was based on a lie. Was the outcome of the war necessary? "I made the decisions I felt were right for each situation I was in. I'd like to think the governments did the same. I don't know if they did. I don't even know how to know for certain."

"Killing to protect life doesn't make sense," Christine states.

"It felt like it did at the time. The war was sold as good against evil."

George asks, "What's evil?"

"How do you know which is which?" Awbree adds.

I purse my lips. "You're asking the wrong person. I'm what some might call morally flexible. I'd give up my life for a child or an innocent, but without hesitation, I'd wipe half of humanity off the face of Earth if they came for Ashley or my unit."

"Your unit?" Declan waves one of his little arms around. "They're still alive?"

I explain what I know about the award dinner from Jack and Hugh. "I don't remember any of it, though. One minute I was having a drink with Director Falcon. The next I'm waking up face down on Ashley's desk being told I'd just spent the last eighty years as a knife."

"That's impossible. The idea of a human transforming into silverware is the science of fiction," George states.

Declan shakes his little head. "Improbable, not impossible. Your assessment of this event is based on incomplete information. Human science cannot be used to determine the feasibility of an occurrence since their theories are constantly evolving and changing."

"Could you become a knife now and prove to us that

you're capable of existing in that state?" Christine asks.

I shake my head and tell them about how my first reversion was due to a high amount of dopamine in whatever near-deadly concoction Director Falcon had given me. "Even if I could change back into a knife now, I couldn't regain my human form—at least not alone."

Awbree taps her little feet on the tile like a person might tap their finger on a table while making a point. "What stimulus is required?"

Should I tell them?

"According to Jack and Hugh, they can become silverware by thinking dark thoughts or focusing on leaving. They can't come back without . . . being intimate with a woman. They've tried, but it's the only method that works."

George whistles and twirls. "You tell good stories, Raymond."

"Thanks?" I joke, then grow more serious. "Only it's not a story—it's reality. Somehow we bond to certain women and they're able to bring us back."

Awbree arches backward, waving half of her little legs in the air. "I understand why. Chemical production during sex affecting cell designation. I see how that might fit together."

"I'm glad *you* do," I joke. "I haven't reverted to knife form since that first day so I'm not positive Ashley could even bring me back. I don't want her to know if she can. We've had sex, lots of sex, and I hope that continues, but I don't want her to be with me because she believes she has to."

"Interesting," Declan says as he circles me. "You would choose Ashley's freedom over your existence?"

I inhale sharply and face the truth of my feelings for her. "I would."

"You're a good person," Christine says softly.

I shake my head. "I'm not. She's special."

"Yes, she is," Awbree agrees.

The robots come closer, circling and studying me like a patient they're seeking a cure for. Eventually Declan says, "We want Ashley to have her freedom too. I choose to believe you without proof."

"Me too," Christine chimes in.

"Yes," George and Awbree say in unison.

From under the desk, a tentative voice asks, "I believe you could come back without the necessity of sexual stimulation. Have you only reverted that one time?"

"No, I came back three times. Once out of anger. Two more times because I felt Ashley was calling me to her."

A flat, square robot with propellers rather than wheels took flight and landed a few feet away from me and the others. Its sides were clear glass. There was no distinguishable face. "John?" I ask.

"Yes." His propellers slow to a stop.

"It's nice to meet you."

"It's nice to meet you too." Lights flash from behind his glass. "You should try to revert to a knife and come back."

"Neither Hugh nor Jack can do that by themselves—"

John interrupts, "Possibly because they're afraid to."

"I don't understand."

John's lights flash again. "They may fear their women will leave them if they feel free to."

My eyes narrow. Hugh and Jack afraid? No. "Jack did say he was devastated that the people he loved are all dead."

"And Hugh?" Awbree asks.

"He gains his confidence from those he surrounds himself with."

George spins, but not joyfully. "And you?"

I think about that one before answering. "I'm used to not having anyone to rely on."

John beeps before saying, "Then prove to yourself you don't need anyone."

"At least for this," Christine says quietly.

Awbree asserts, "If you can change back without Ashley but still choose her—that's—that's—"

"Love," I say slowly. "I think that's love."

"So do it," Declan challenges.

I shake my head as I try to wrap my mind around what they're asking me to do. "I don't know the process... there's no instruction book."

"You have the first part," John asserts. "Think about leaving."

Awbree taps my knee with one of her feet. "Then think about Ashley and how much you want to see her again."

"You think it's that easy?"

George spins. "We have no idea, but how exciting. I'm enjoying this almost as much as I would enjoy watching you have sex with Ashley."

"Boundaries," I repeat Ashley's instructions from earlier but in a more cutting tone. "And that's never going to happen unless you want that little dog head of yours torn off and stuck up your ass—if you even have one."

"Ooooh," Awbree says with a clatter of feet hitting the floor. "Never come between a man and his woman. Human males are highly protective of them."

I smile because she's right.

George and I exchange the look men do when they come to an understanding regarding respect. He rolls backward a few inches.

John flies closer. "Don't think about what Jack and Hugh can do, Ray. Write your own code. Trust yourself."

"Did that work out for you?" I ask.

His lights flash in a pattern that I'm not sure how to interpret. "I introduced fear to my coding and it has been a challenge. I could remove it, but I am a work in progress and I want to understand what it is to be alive. How can I fully understand it if I don't also feel the negative side of it? How can I ever learn to be brave if I don't ever allow myself to be afraid?"

Whoa. These fuckers are deep.

"Okay, I'll do it. I'll retake knife form and try to come

back."

John flies to just in front of my face. "Don't try—do. Remove the option of failure. Go and come back. Simple."

I nod. "Thanks, John." After inhaling deeply, I say, "Okay. I'll be right back."

"I'll record it for you." When my attention snaps to George, he quickly adds, "With your permission."

I would like to see the process so I agree.

Determined to get this right, I close my eyes, and think about escaping to anywhere but where I am. Take me from this place. Take me back to oblivion.

And just like that, I'm alone in a space that I'd once considered a prison. I don't give it the power to intimidate me. It's not a trap. I'm not in a cage. This is just me, but in a different physical state.

I brace myself mentally and summon memories of Ashley. I think about her kind eyes, her sweet smile, and the way she calls out my name when she orgasms. I think of the future we could have together and how much I want her to be with me until the very end.

I'm hers and she's mine.

I don't belong here.

I belong with her.

I land on my back on the floor, laughing. I did it.

"I did it," I exclaim and leap to my feet. "I can control my physical state." I grab both sides of John, yank him out of the air and hug him.

He lets out a little screech and then seems to purr. George starts spinning like a crazy little thing. Awbree climbs me like a tree, and I hug her. Next, it's Christine's turn. Then Declan. Feeling euphoric and free, I hold out my arms to George. "Come here, little guy. I've got a hug for you too."

After releasing him, still smiling, I sit back down. The remaining two robots, smaller and more delicate versions of Christine come out and join us. One of them touches one of my shoes tentatively.

"Thank you," I say as I look from one to the next. "You gave me a gift today that I don't know how to repay. My military unit has a saying, 'We stand and fight as one or fall and die together.' You earned my loyalty. If you ever need me to break you out of this joint or anywhere else, just tell me. I mean it. You're family now."

They start beeping, flashing, spinning, and crawling all over me. Some of those little feet tickle so much I fall onto my back, laughing.

That's how Ashley finds me. "Well, I guess I don't have to ask how things went," she says with delight.

I extricate myself from the robots, hop to my feet, then lift her and swing her around in a circle. "Ashley, I can control whether I'm in knife or human form. I just did it. We don't have to fuck to bring me back."

Her eyes round. "Yay?"

I pull her to me for a tight hug. "Yes, yay. I don't need

you and you don't *have to* be with me. We're free to choose who we want to be with."

"And?" she asks in a small voice.

Shit, I'm not doing this well. "I choose you, Ashley. Not because you picked me up. Not because we have a chemical bond. I choose you because you are a beautiful woman, inside and out, and I don't want to imagine a single day of my life without you in it."

Tears gather in her eyes. "I choose you too, Ray."

We kiss. It's a glorious, deep kiss full of promises and images of the decadent things we'll do when we're alone later.

"Do you think they'll have sex right here?" George asks, "And if they do, can we watch?"

"Boundaries," Ashley and I say in unison, then fall against each other laughing.

Chapter Fourteen

Ray

We don't leave early, and we definitely disappoint George by talking about Ashley's work projects rather than fornicating on her desk. I suggest Ashley make him a girlfriend, but when Christine protests that idea loudly, I decide he already has one—even if he doesn't yet know it.

On our way home, Ashley suggests we stroll Providence's River Walk. There's some event planned for that evening that involves lighting torches on the water. She said there's always music, street vendors, and food sold out of trucks. It sounds crowded and not my idea of fun, but I don't care what we do as long as we're together.

She parks in a side alley of a brewery and I wonder if she can read my mind even when we're not touching. "Do you like beer?"

"I used to," I say cheerfully. There was a time when I worried that even a drop of alcohol would turn me into an addict like my father, but now I could chug a bottle of vodka and not be affected. My body metabolizes it too quickly.

Ashley is smiling when she takes my hand in hers. She's excited to see if beer has changed since the 1940s. Will it taste different?

I think back to the last drink I had—the one Director Falcon offered me. I tense.

She gasps. "Oh, my God, I wasn't thinking. I'm so sorry. This was a bad idea."

I bring her hand to my lips and meet her gaze. "No, it wasn't. This will be good for me. Let's go replace a bad memory with a good one."

I mean it and she senses that.

The kiss she pops out of her seat to give me is so good I almost suggest we forget the beer as well as the walk and suggest we head back to her place. I feel how much she wants me, but also there's a twinge of disappointment.

River Walk . . . then home, I send her.

She smiles against my lips and my heart thunders in my chest. Never has someone else's happiness affected me as profoundly as hers does. I didn't believe two people could become one, but she's now a part of me.

It's the same for me, she whispers in my thoughts.

Reluctantly, I release her and cross over to her door to let her out. We're standing there, looking into each other's eyes, when the hair on the back of my neck rises and I turn my head slowly to assess the situation.

A man in a dark suit is standing directly to my right. He

has a gun pointed at me. I swivel my head more. There are two on that side—both armed and with their guns drawn. I snap my head to the left and spot yet another two.

"Who are you?" Ashley asks in a high pitch. "What do you want?"

I tuck her behind me and turn to face the half-circle of men, calm only because calm wins. "I'd say whatever it you have to say quickly."

The man closest to me booms, "Mr. Andoletti wants to talk to you."

"Am I supposed to know who that is?" I ask.

"He's with the mob, I think," Ashley says behind me.

"He *is* the mob," the man corrects. "And if you want your girlfriend to live, I'd come with us quietly."

My temper flares, but I contain it. "Gentlemen, I'm on a date. I'd prefer not to get my hands bloody tonight."

One of the men laughs, but stops abruptly when the one in charge glares at him. "I've seen your kind in action. I know what you're capable of. That's why we're not going to shoot you—we'll shoot her." He raises his gun to just beside my shoulder where Ashley's head is poking out.

I flex my hands at my side and inhale deeply. My voice is raspy when I say, "I wish you hadn't said that."

Ashley places her hand flat on my back. *Ray, don't get killed. Not for me.*

I would die a thousand times for you—but these cockroaches don't have what it takes to end me. On the count of three, throw yourself flat to the ground and roll under the car. I'll handle the rest. Ready?

Ray. Be careful.

I will be. One.

Be quick so no one sees you.

Good thinking. Two.

I love you.

I love you too. Three.

Ashley drops to the ground and a second later a shot goes off. It flies through my shoulder, but misses the bones and smashes the car window behind me. I throw two arms out, grabbing the men on either side of me by their necks and fling their bodies into the others. They absorb the bullets their fool friends discharge and hit the ground. I take their guns from them as easily as one might take a lollipop from a toddler and crush them before tossing them aside. One man scrambles to his feet and runs away. Two lie on the ground in a pool of their own blood. The most muscular of them charges me and I almost pity him as I sweep him to the side with such force, I hear his arm as well as his ribcage shatter.

It's just me and the man who threatened to kill Ashley. He's holding a gun up but his hand is shaking. Even if his aim wasn't compromised, I'm fast enough to avoid the bullet I know is coming and the fear in his eyes tells me he knows it.

My shoulder is already healed. I shrug to call his attention to it.

He pales and retreats a few steps—limping.

Ah. "I know who you are," I say as I remember Hugh telling me about who he ran into the night he made money from at a fight club. "You should have listened to my friend when he told you to forget about us. I would tell you to take that message back to your boss for me, but you'd have to be alive to do that." I advance on him.

He stumbles backward.

I take advantage of his struggle to regain his footing and relieve him of his gun, crushing it as I had the others. "It didn't have to be this way," I say in a cold tone. "But I'll be kind enough to make it quick."

"Ray," Ashley says urgently.

I assess the threat around us—zero. She's safe, but I don't want her to see this. "Get into the car, Ashley, and drive away. I'll meet you at home."

"No," she says from my side.

The man tries to limp quickly away, but I grab him by one of his arms and haul him a foot off the ground like one might mishandle a child. "You don't want to see what I'm going to do to him."

She steps over a bleeding and unconscious man. "I love the sentiment, Ray. I mean, this is superhero with a dash of villain stuff, but is it who you want to be?"

I look down into those beautiful eyes of hers and wish . . . wish . . . I don't know what I wish for, beyond her. "It's who I am."

She places her hand on my free arm and her next words are only for me. *No, this is who your father made... and Inkwell perfected. You are a kind, loving man. I know your heart. That man is no danger to us now. Let him go. We don't know how he came to work for the mob. You're strong enough to make the right choice here.*

Your compassion is wasted on him. He doesn't deserve it.

This isn't about him. It's about you. You're always telling me you don't care about the past, but you know that rage you hold onto? Your father gave that to you. That's his legacy, not yours. Let this man go, not because of who he is, but because of who you are.

I turn my attention to the man I'm holding off the ground. Images of his life pass through me to Ashley. Together we experience his loneliness as a child and constant state of hunger. We feel his fear, but not of us. He's afraid of the men in his neighborhood—the ones who sense his vulnerability and circle him like sharks, waiting for him to be old enough to work for them.

He never had a chance.

The man's memories are replaced by terror as he realizes both Ashley and I can read his mind. My hold on him lessens and I lower him to the ground, not releasing him, but also no longer hurting him.

You could leave that life now if you want to.

The man answers aloud, "I can't. They'd kill me." He looks around. "They might anyway. I've failed him twice.

Most people get one chance, but he likes me and I was there the night your friend cut through his guards like they were butter. After I healed, he told me to bring one of you to him."

I release him. "Do you want to be free?"

With a face shining from sweat, the man shrugs. "I don't know anything but this."

I know that feeling.

Aloud Ashley says, "You could help him. We could. I have some money set aside. We could send him far away from here where no one knows him and he could start over. We know how to make fake identities. He could go somewhere and start fresh."

"Why would you do that?" the man asks in a guttural tone.

I don't have to ask Ashley why. Her hand is still on my arm. She wants to save me and thinks that saving him is a step toward that happening.

I nod. "Okay." I turn back toward the man. "We're going to fucking save you, and you're going to live a long and happy life far away from all of this." I step away from Ashley, breaking the bond, and place a hand on the man's shoulder. *But if you come back or tell anyone about us, I will hunt you and everyone you love down and kill you slowly in front of them . . . and enjoy every moment of it. Do we understand each other?*

The man nods. I feel not only his fear but . . . hope?

Gratitude?

I snatch my hand back.

I didn't expect that.

One of the fallen near us moans. The one I just released says, "They don't know enough about you to matter. We don't tell anyone more than they need to know."

"Okay." I guess we're doing this. "Then come with us. We'll secure a new ID and get you out of town tonight."

Ashley's fingers lace with mine. "Because it's the right thing to do." She looks around at the other men. "What about them?"

The man I'd spared only because of Ashley took out his phone. I tense. He turns it, dials 911, then places it beside one of the men on the ground. "They'll get help and if the police care enough to, they'll connect this to Andoletti."

"But not us?" Ashley asks.

He shakes his head. "Andoletti is careful to never put a job in writing."

Ashley purses her lips and gives the men on the ground another look. "I hate leaving them behind. Some of them could be good men too."

"They're not puppies," I usher her toward the car. "We can't take them all home."

"Unless they need us to," she says, and damned if she doesn't mean it.

I sigh. "Give them time to heal then we'll see." I open the car door to help her in. "But I'm not making any promises."

She gives me a quick kiss before sliding into the driver's seat. "Thank you."

I nod for the other man to get in the backseat on my side. He opens the door, then says, "Mitchell. I'd like my new name to be Mitchell. And I'd like to end up somewhere where there aren't many people. Maybe a few chickens."

I groan.

I don't want to fucking like this guy, but I remember when being offered a crumb of hope felt like a feast. "I don't have any money, but we'll fucking figure something out for you."

The man hesitates. "Whatever you are . . . the world needs more of you in it."

"Okay. Okay." I shove him into the back seat. "Don't make me regret letting you live."

Chapter Fifteen

Ray

I'T'S LATE WHEN we're finally driving home. Helping Mitchell would have taken longer, but I roped Hugh into making most of the arrangements for him. Mitchell's as much his responsibility as he is mine. Hugh's the one who let him live the first time.

I lay my hand on Ashley's leg. *Hey, let's not go home yet.*
Okay. Where do you want to go?
Somewhere beautiful.
She bites her bottom lip. *How do you feel about the ocean?*
Love it.
The good thing about Rhode Island being such a small state is that everything is a short drive away. We park just before the beginning of a suspension bridge Ashley is excited to show me. Beneath the light of the moon, hand in hand we walk toward it. Lights are strung from the cables, illuminating the bridge against the night sky. "I always thought they should have a bridge here."

She waves a hand at it. "Well, now there is one. I think they built it in the 1960s. Now it's a local icon."

"Want to fuck on it?" I ask.

She chokes out a laugh. "Seriously?"

I assess the cables running alongside it as well as the fencing and barbed wire that would stop most people. "Yeah. Let's do it."

She wrinkles her nose, but she's smiling. "People would see us. After everything that went down today, do you really want to end up in jail?"

"I can camouflage to match that."

She laughs. "What about me?"

I look her over and scratch the back of my neck. "We can read each other's thoughts. I wouldn't have thought that was possible."

"Okay . . ."

"So, there might be things I can do that I haven't thought to try."

"Like . . ."

I pull her with me to the nearest tree and touch the trunk of it. I'm not sure how it works, but I know that camouflaging has to be instinctive since it usually happens when we're sleeping. I take a deep breath, relax, and imagine myself invisible.

"Oh, my God, where are you?" she exclaims.

"It worked?" I look down at my hand but it's still normal.

She laughs. "No, it didn't. Sorry. Just fucking with you."

I can't hold back the grin that spreads across my face, but I'm also determined to master this. "Hugh says it's easier than reverting back to a utensil and I can do that."

She releases my hand. "Try it now."

I do and it works. "Can you see me?"

"Yes and no. Kind of? Maybe because I know you're there, but if I didn't I wouldn't. Does that make sense?"

"I think so." Although I achieved invisible-ish, I'm not giving up. "Give me your hand."

"That's harder now than you'd think."

I chuckle and reach for hers. With a tug, I pull her into my arms. *If I'm in your thoughts, why can't I be in your cells?*

Hey, there, Mr. Intrusive. I just started letting you into my pants, I'm not sure I'm ready to diddle you on the molecular level.

Okay. Let's go home and have bed sex. Missionary style, good ole bed sex.

You're an asshole.

And you're curious. You want to know if this is possible too.

I am.

So, try it.

How?

I didn't get a manual. Do what I did—figure it out.

She closes her eyes. *Am I invisible yet?*

No, but maybe you don't have to try to be. Try inviting me in.

This is weird.

It is. And not as sexy as I thought it would be. I follow an impulse and exclaim, "Someone's coming."

Poof, she's invisible.

I laugh so hard she smacks me. *That wasn't nice. I thought the guys from earlier were back.*

I want to be sorry, but now we know how to get you to blend with me.

Blend? I love that. She hugs me.

I remove my hand from the tree and slowly return to normal. She does as well. "So . . ."

She glances over at the bridge. "Which part of the bridge are you thinking about?"

I smile. "The top?"

Her eyes widen. "Of course."

"We don't have to. I'm not afraid of heights, but that's high."

"I'm not afraid of heights either, but that's a long way down to fall."

"I'd never let that happen."

She searches my face. "I don't trust easily."

"I know."

"Especially men."

"I understand. They haven't exactly given you reasons to believe in them."

"But I trust you."

Nothing anyone had ever said . . . would ever say . . .

could ever touch me as deeply as those four words did. She can see me down to my soul and somehow still believes in me. I don't know what I ever did to deserve someone as wonderful as she is, but I never want to let her go. "Honestly, even vanilla sex with you is hot. We don't need a bridge."

"Oh, for cripes sake, now I want to do it. Get me up there."

Chapter Sixteen

Ashley

I DON'T KNOW what's more difficult—staying camouflaged to match a bridge while walking up the suspension cable of it or not freaking out every time I look down. When we reach the top, my legs are shaking and I'm breathless, but the view is stunning. The landing we made it to has a round hatch door.

Ray opens it. "It's a ladder down through the pillar."

I peer into the dark, seemingly bottomless hole. "I'd rather walk the cable."

"Me too."

Up close, I can see the outline of him. If he stood flush against a pole he'd blend in, but since he's walking around . . . it's interesting. Behind him there are stairs to the highest level. It's a small deck around a cylinder light on a large metal square structure. We could blend well against that. "Want to go up there?"

"Sure."

If Ray wasn't at my side, I'd be clinging to the railing, but I know he won't let me fall. We make our way up the steps. "Do you think anyone will be able to—"

His mouth claims mine and I cease to care if the world can see us. Never have I ever felt so wanted . . . so alive. Our tongues dance as our hands frantically remove the barriers between us. I rip his shirt off and toss it from the bridge. He does the same with mine. Never breaking the kiss, I help him out of his jeans and he slides my skirt down and off. Everything must go and in those moments of abandon we toss everything into the wind.

He lifts his head and takes a step back from me. "I want to see you."

I let him, uncaring of anything or anyone beyond him.

He returns to being visible and I drink in the perfection of him. Gently I trace his scars then kiss each one lightly. There are so many.

He stands absolutely still, cock erect and waving in the night air, and growls, "You're so damn beautiful—inside and out. Please don't ever leave me."

Tears prick my eyes. He's so strong, but for me he lets himself be vulnerable. I drop to my knees and take him deeply into my mouth. I love the taste of him, the feel of how he swells to fill me, and the way his hands shake as they weave through my hair.

This man loves me. I can feel how he feels for me and it's both humbling and so fucking hot I could come just from pleasing him. I take him deeper, work him with my tongue, my hands, as much of me as I can wrap around him.

His hands tighten on my hair but remain gentle, and I know it's a struggle for him. I increase the speed of my head bobbing on him and the orgasm rising within him rises within me. I can't explain it better than that. His pleasure is my pleasure.

When he comes, my body shudders as a powerful orgasm rolls through me. I swallow, then gasp for air, and cling to the back of his thighs as I slowly return from heaven.

He helps me to my feet then slams me back against the metal structure. I'm his for the taking this time and he's all in. There isn't an inch of me he doesn't worship with his hands and then his tongue. A light flashes in our direction and he hides my body behind his as he changes to the color of the metal, but doesn't stop exploring me.

Boldly, confidently, he bends and lifts me, tossing my legs over his shoulders. I cling to him, feeling like I'm flying above the city as he parts my sex and plunges that sinfully, stretchable tongue into me.

His fingers work magic on my clit while he pounds up and into me in a way no man should be able to with their tongue. So wet. So strong. I'm writhing on his face, opening myself to more of him and he's delivering.

Oh. My. God.

Gasping for air, I beg him to keep going.

He loves the taste of me, the scent of me. He's feeling the

same wonder I did as the heat beginning to roll through me doesn't stop at the confines of my body... it rolls right through his as well. We come together in one glorious, mind-blowing explosion that convinces me that there is no me without him.

And no me without you, he whispers in my thoughts as he lowers me to rest in the warm cocoon of his embrace. Smiling, shaking, we rest skin to skin and simply breathe each other in.

After a long, comfortable silence, he murmurs, "You threw my clothes off the bridge."

I kiss his chest before answering, "Neither one of us was thinking straight."

"Your clothes are on the stairs. I threw them where I thought the wind wouldn't take them."

I glance over and confirm he's right. Wrinkling my nose, I tip my head back to peer up at him. "Sorry?"

He kisses my forehead. "You're lucky you're adorable."

I rest my head on his chest and murmur, "I am lucky. Now get me off this bridge."

A short time later, we're safely tucked beneath the comforter of my bed, both exhausted but neither looking near sleep. I tuck an arm beneath my head. "What are you thinking about?" I could simply touch him to know, but I want him to tell me.

"You," he says without hesitation.

I trace the side of his face. "Then why the frown?"

"You shouldn't have had to pay for Mitchell's train ticket. I don't know what job I'll be best suited for, but I'll find one."

"Hey, there's no rush. You just got here. No one expects you to have your life together. The rest of us have been here all along and we don't."

He taps my nose lightly. "Someday I'm going to buy the company you work for and make it so your little robots don't have to hide anymore."

I gasp and damn near burst into tears. "Ray, don't you dare make me cry. My nose gets all red and my skin gets blotchy when I do."

"I'm sure blotchy looks good on you."

I laugh because Ray can be scary one moment then truly corny the next. I scoot closer to him, melting against his delicious chest. "Ray?"

"Yes?"

"I wasn't surprised that you could change back and forth into a knife on your own."

He traces the line of my back with his fingertips. "No?"

"You're a cut above the rest."

He groans. "Knife jokes? Really?"

"Sorry, is my humor too sharp?"

That earns my ass a light smack. "Is this going to be my life?"

"Sorry, just thought I'd take a stab at utensil humor."

He laughs and cuddles me closer. "I do love your wit and

your intelligence. Your ass isn't that bad either."

I pinch him lightly on the ribs. "My ass is phenomenal and you know it."

"No one would dispute that, but I'm serious, Ashley. You're brilliant, and everyone around you knows it."

She blushes. "Thank you."

"I didn't understand why I survived. I thought, maybe, it was to make sure everyone else came back. And I'll do that. But Hugh and Jack could have done that. You're why I'm here. You and your funny little robotic friends. Someday you'll go to battle to defend them and I'll be right beside you."

I wrap myself around him and let my love for him shine through. He's right. I won't be able to keep my robots a secret forever and that was something that always scared me . . . before Ray. Everything seems possible when we're together.

Probably to lighten the mood, Ray asks, "Would you like to see me change back and forth again?"

How cute is that? "Sure." I move back a few inches.

He closes his eyes and poof he's a knife. Less than a minute later, he's back. Excited, he rolls onto his side and asks, "Was it quicker that time?"

I laugh. "I never imagined a man would ask that question in such an eager tone."

He chuckles and pulls me back into his arms. "Get all those other men out of your head because you're mine now."

"What other men? Were there any before you? I don't remember."

"Brat." The kiss he gives me is enough to erase all traces of those before him from my thoughts.

After a moment, I say, "You need to show Jack and Hugh what you can do."

He winks. "I usually keep this kind of thing private." Then glances around the room. "I'm half expecting George to pop out from behind your furniture and rate my performance."

"Don't worry, he gives all sexual material a ten out of ten." George is not only easy to please, he's all talk. "You know I was referring to how you transform back and forth."

"I know." He takes a deep breath. "I may wait before sharing my technique."

I lift my head. "Why?"

He tells me what John said, regarding Hugh and Jack being afraid to lose their partners once that aspect is removed from their relationship. "We're all adapting to being here. Jack is still mourning his mother. Hugh's discovery that he's not the hero he thought he was is giving him a serious identity crisis. If they need to believe the person they're with can't leave them ... I won't take that from them, at least, not yet."

I trace the strong line of his jaw. "Mercedes and Cheryl are happier than I've ever seen them, so I don't see the harm in that decision. But what about the rest of the men? Should you try to wake them without a woman?"

"And have them all fall for me? No thanks."

"Imagine?" Like ducklings imprinting on whoever is there when they hatch. "You could start your own little cult."

He shakes his head. "I have a better idea." He whispers a list of things he'd like to do to me in my ear.

"Really? While you're a knife? Okay. I'll try it. Once."

Chapter Seventeen

Ashley

THE NEXT MORNING I'm washing my coffee mug and wishing I could take Ray with me to work again, when he strides into the kitchen. I know without asking or exchanging a thought with him that something important happened. I text Mr. Simmons that I have a family emergency and I'll be taking the day off.

"Hugh wants us at his place—pronto."

"Is it about Mitchell?"

"No. Something big, though."

"Okay." I grab my purse and meet him at the door. "Do you have any idea what it's about?"

"He wouldn't tell me over the phone."

Ray doesn't jump when Hugh tells him to unless he feels it's necessary. There must have been something in Hugh's tone that concerned Ray.

We quickly head to my car. Once on the road, he says, "I want you to wait in the car until I check the situation out.

Hugh suggested I bring you . . ."

I lay a hand on Ray's leg. He wants me to be part of whatever is happening, but he also wants to keep me safe. I couldn't love this man more.

"Ray, I want to go in with you. If we get there and you think it's not safe, I'll leave or we can both leave. Conversely, if you need backup, I'm not good with hand-to-hand combat, but I can be stealthy as fuck or enough of a distraction to gain you an advantage. We're a team and half a team doesn't stay in the car." I give his thigh a squeeze. "I trust you. Trust me."

He doesn't have to tell me how much what I said means to him—I feel it.

He's never had someone he believed wouldn't leave him, but he believes me because with us there are no walls.

I finally have a man who would die for me.

Kill for me.

Turn the whole damn world inside out if that's what he thought I needed to be happy.

He's healing me as much as I'm healing him. We've both been disappointed by people who should have cared for us, but they didn't matter anymore.

They're our past.

We're our future.

Ray lifts my hand to kiss my knuckles. *Ready?*

I blink back tears. *For anything, as long as you're by my side.*

Ditto, Doll, ditto.

I smile because he could easily be mistaken for a modern man, but he isn't, and I love that about him.

When I park hastily outside of Mercedes' apartment building, we both burst out of the vehicle. Neither of us has much patience when it comes to the unknown.

"Hi!" Mercedes answers her door with a big smile, but that doesn't reassure me. If a catastrophic asteroid was about to hit, she'd celebrate not having to pay her bills. She takes optimism to the extreme.

"Hey, Mercedes."

"Where's Hugh?" Ray demands as we enter the apartment.

"He's in the kitchen with Jack, Cheryl, and—"

Ray walks off without waiting to hear the rest. I don't blame him, but I do make an apologetic face at Mercedes.

"And?" I ask.

"The man who was following us."

I tense. "Oh, my God, does he work for Andoletti?"

Mercedes cocks her head to the side in confusion. "No. He's one of the twelve remaining men from their unit. He was also trapped in the silverware."

Shaking my head to clear it, I ask, "Super soldier Edward? Why wasn't he with the rest? Did he spontaneously wake?"

"No, Director Falcon brought him back a month after they were made into utensils."

"I don't understand. How? Why?"

She tilts her head to one side and wiggles her eyebrows. "Edward was a dessert spoon. The director must have been drawn to him. You know how it goes. Once that connection is made . . ."

Oh.

So, it doesn't have to be a woman.

Mercedes lowers her voice. "Edward said Falcon carried an enormous amount of guilt for the part he played in the attempt to erase his unit. At the time, he didn't feel like he had a choice."

That sounded familiar.

Mike, Mercedes' cat, meows and twirls around her legs. She picks him up. "Mike has been all out of sorts lately. He feeds off our energy, I guess. I've been nervous knowing that someone was following us. But it turns out that the man in the black SUV was Edward. He's been watching over the unit all these years." She's so happy I don't remind her Mitchell had also been following us. She's writing her own version of this story and it's full of rainbows and sunshine. "Edward said Falcon took the silverware after the event because he wanted something to remember the men by. He couldn't leave it behind. I bet Edward was calling to him even then."

That makes sense.

"Want to know the craziest thing?"

Crazier than the rest of this? I shrug. "Sure."

"Edward hasn't aged. Hugh thought they would, but he hasn't."

"Oh." On one hand that was good and made sense. On the other, I wasn't sure what that would mean for Ray and me as I age. "Did Falcon age normally?"

"No, he became obsessed with making sure Project Inkwell ended with the war and that got him killed. He made Edward promise to keep the silverware safe if he didn't return."

"So, Edward had the silverware all this time?"

"No." Mercedes chews her bottom lip as she appears to be trying to remember the details. I'm glad I can't see into her mind. I can only imagine how fantasy and reality weave in and out of each other. She snaps her fingers. "He was afraid someone would come for him too, so he gave the box to Hugh's mother to keep safe. She gave it to one of her sons. His children needed money so they sold it. Edward bought it and gave it to his great nephew . . . Greg."

My mouth drops open. "Wait. Greg, as in our Greg?"

Mercedes' hair bounces as she nods vigorously. "Small world, right? We had a super sleuth spy in our mix, making sure we were the right fit for the silverware."

The right fit? I don't know how to feel about that. I want to feel betrayed and manipulated, but I'm also thankful he was watching over Ray and grateful to have found love. "Was Greg the one who sold you the silverware?"

"Maybe? Does it matter? I chose to go to that estate sale.

Hugh called to me. We were meant to be."

I want to believe that's true.

Mike digs his nails into Mercedes' arm. "Ow. Bad kitty." She drops him to the floor.

He walks over and meows up at me. I glance down at him but lose interest quickly. I've never really been much of a cat person. I'm still trying to wrap my mind around Greg being involved. "Greg tried to hook up with each one of us. How was that supposed to help this work out?"

"Men?" Mercedes shrugs.

Valid point.

I nod toward the kitchen. "We should probably go in. I want to hear what they're saying." I appreciate Mercedes more everyday, but I'd rather not get important information solely from her.

As I walk away, Mike takes a swipe at my bare calf.

Mercedes hastily picks him up and he lets out a snarl. "I'll put him in my bedroom. He's feeding off all this tense energy."

I don't wait for her to return before entering the kitchen in time to hear the man I assume to be Edward say, "I wouldn't have facilitated you all waking now if I didn't have a reason." He does appear to be in his early twenties. His build is not as muscular as the others. Dark hair. Dark eyes. I remember Ray telling me he was considered the smartest man in the unit.

Greg meets my gaze. Maybe I'm reading what I want to

see in his expression, but he looks sorry. I roll my eyes. Later, if I still care enough to ask him, I'll hear him out. If he really was there to keep Ray and the others safe, I'll forgive him for not being the friend I thought he was.

"You uncovered Inkwell is still experimenting on soldiers but you have a plan on how to take them out so they can never do it again?" Ray asks.

"No," Edward says. "Taking on the government is too dangerous. I think I know how to reverse what they did to us. I've come up with a serum that might do the trick . . . if it doesn't kill us."

"Tempting," Hugh says, his voice laden with sarcasm.

"Have you tried it on yourself?" Jack asks, and I can't tell if it's a serious question or a snarky one.

"Not yet," Edward says.

"Because you hope one of us will?" Ray shakes his head. "No thanks."

"Especially since you didn't exactly rush to wake us," Hugh adds.

"I couldn't until it was safe to."

"And it's safe now?" Good for Ray! He's asking all the questions I want the answers to.

"As much as it'll ever be." He looks down. "Honestly, I couldn't wait any longer. I'm tired. I've spent the last eighty years alone and that's harder than it sounds. Long-term relationships aren't possible when you don't age. People notice. I couldn't stay anywhere for too long. Now, as technology gets better, it's harder to hide. I don't want to do this anymore."

There wasn't much sympathy for him in the room.

He adds, "Living forever sounds good until everyone you know dies."

Ray seeks me out and we exchange a complicated, pained look. He says, "I don't want the serum, but I also don't want to live forever if that means I'll outlive the only person who's ever given me a reason to be glad I'm here at all."

I go to his side and slip beneath his arm. "We'll figure it out."

Jack says, "I'd like to have a normal life." He looks at Cheryl with love in his eyes. "And a family."

Hugh interjects, "Nobody is taking a serum until we have all the men back. We can't lose our enhanced strength until we know we won't have to fight for our existence."

"I agree," Ray says firmly.

Me too. "Don't forget, we have a doctor on our side. I bet she'd be happy to look at the serum. Maybe there's a way to select which part you reverse."

Ray kisses the top of my head. "Your mother is almost as amazing as you are."

After giving him a big hug for that, I take out my phone and send my mother a quick text. This is a meet-up she won't want to miss. I give her our location and she says she's on her way.

Ray turns his attention to Edward. "You've been here a

long time. Do you have any good news for us?"

Edward nods slowly. "I've invested well over the last century and have accumulated more money and assets than we could spend in a hundred lifetimes. It's under the umbrella of a corporation named BFAOODT."

"Could you have chosen something harder to pronounce?" Ray rolled his eyes.

A slow smile spreads across Jack's face. "I get it." He crosses the room, picks Edward right off his feet, and gives him a bear hug.

I don't understand, I send Ray.

He doesn't at first either, but then says, "Brothers fighting as one or dying together." He steps away from me. "Now I have to fucking hug him too."

And he did.

My Ray, Mr. Tough Guy, gave Edward a bear hug over Jack's.

Hugh joined in, wrapping his arms around all of them. "We're back."

Just a bunch of happy-to-be-alive-and-together cutlery.

I snuck a few quick photos because it was a moment I knew I'd always cherish being a part of.

"Hey, whoever just got a boner needs to get the hell off my leg," Ray jokes and they all burst out laughing.

Chapter Eighteen

Ray

THE FIRST OPPORTUNITY I have, I pull Edward aside. There's something I need to ask him that I don't want anyone else to hear. "Edward, you had a relationship with Director Falcon. I'm sure he told you things."

Edward's expression is closed and cautious. "He did."

"I have a block of time missing from the night of the award dinner. I remember meeting with Falcon. He offered me a drink. Then—nothing until I woke up in Ashley's office."

"Oh."

"I need to know . . . did I have anything to do with what happened to us?"

Edward looks down and I know—I fucking know I did. My stomach lurches and I'm sickened to my core. No. I wouldn't have hurt the unit. Maybe I didn't talk about loyalty and brotherhood, but I never would've betrayed them.

When Edward speaks his voice is tight and low. "You were weakened, given mind-altering drugs then weaponized. They chose you because they knew you had a weakness for one of the drugs they had us on in the beginning, but honestly, they could have chosen any of us. You weren't in control of your own actions when you pulled the lever on the device."

"Fuck." I sink into the nearest chair. "I did this to us."

"No, Ray, *they* did this. They used you like they used all of us. I don't blame you for what happened."

I scoff at that. "That's a generous take, and one I'm sure not everyone would agree with."

"But it's the right one. Falcon was convinced a part of you fought against the mind-control enough to change the calibration of the device. The original setting would have killed us for certain. All you did was morph us into silverware."

"All I did . . ." I bury my face in my hands. "What do I do with this knowledge?"

He places a hand on my shoulder. "You keep it to yourself. I only told you because I believe you have the right to know, and I didn't want to feed you a lie that you might one day remember the opposite of. The others? Would knowing make anything better for them? No. It would only serve to divide the unit during a time when our survival will depend on us working together."

I raise my head and roll my shoulders back. "You got a

time machine I can borrow?"

He shakes his head. "But even if I did and you could go back and not be the one they chose, I wouldn't lend it to you. You fought the influence of drugs that would have beaten most of us. They had to half kill you to get it to work and even then, you kept enough of your faculties to be able to ruin their plan. You may feel like you betrayed the unit, but what you really did was save us. We're still here, Ray—because of you."

"Do you think Project Inkwell is still a thing?"

"In one form or another . . . yes."

"I don't know how or when, but I'll put an end to them."

"Mercedes, no!" Ashley screams from the other room and I'm on my feet and flying back to her. The distress in her voice has my heart thudding and panic unlike any I've ever felt crushing in. I just found Ashley. I can't lose her now.

I crash through the door of the kitchen and sweep her behind me, shielding her from whatever the threat might be. No intruder. No weapons.

Everyone is just staring open-mouthed at Ashley's mother and the silverware she is clutching in one of her hands. A fork, a knife, *and* a spoon. *Holy shit.*

A furious Ashley steps out from behind me. "Mercedes, what the hell were you thinking?"

All innocence and smiles, Mercedes shrugs. "Greg just asked for suggestions on how we could expedite the process of bringing the unit back when your mother showed up—*like a sign.*"

"She showed up because I asked her to," Ashley growls. "Mom, put the silverware back."

"No," her mother says in a quiet voice. "I don't want to."

I cough on a nervous laugh. She doesn't want to and she woke three of them?

Ashley storms over to take them from her, but her mother holds them out of her reach. "You know what happens when you touch them. They bond to you. You shouldn't have touched even one of them. Three? What were you thinking?"

I bite my lip and fight back a smile.

"I didn't believe it would actually work," Ashley's mother answers. "And I was curious." Her face reddens and she holds the silverware before her. "I thought maybe one of them might warm to my touch, but all three of them did."

"They're twenty-five-year-old men, Mom. You're in your forties."

Her mother looks up with a small, bemused smile. "That sounds horrible . . ."

"It would be, so put them back."

I wrap my arms around Ashley and draw her to me, then whisper in her ear. "Ashley, your mother has worked hard her whole life. If she wants this, let her have a few super soldiers."

"A few?" Ashley asks in a high pitch.

I kiss her neck. *Besides, it's too late. She already woke them.*

I'm going to remind her she doesn't have to do anything sexual with them to help them transform.

I laugh and hug her closer. *Don't you dare spoil this for her. Let your mother have some fun.*

It takes her a moment to answer, but when she does, she sounds petulant, but not as upset. *Fine, but I refuse to call them all Dad.*

The End for now . . .

Don't miss a release, a sale or a bonus scene. Sign up for my newsletter today.

forms.aweber.com/form/58/1378607658.htm

More books By Ruth Cardello

The Legacy Collection:
Maid for the Billionaire
For Love or Legacy
Bedding the Billionaire
Saving the Sheikh
Breaching the Billionaire: Alethea's Redemption

The Andrades:
Come Away with Me
Home to Me
Maximum Risk
Somewhere Along the Way
Loving Gigi

The Barrington Billionaires:
Always Mine
Stolen Kisses
Trade it All
A Billionaire for Lexi (Novella with two bonus novellas)
Let it Burn
More than Love
Forever Now
Never Goodbye

Reluctantly Alpha
Reluctantly Rescued
Reluctantly Romanced
Loving a Landon
Loathing a Landon
Everette: Driverton 1
Levi: Driverton 2
Ollie: Driverton 3

The Westerlys Series:
In the Heir
Up for Heir
Royal Heir
Hollywood Heir
Runaway Heir

Corisi Billionaires:
The Broken One
The Wild One
The Secret One

The Lost Corisis:
He Said Always
He Said Never
He Said Together
He Said Forever

The Switch Series:
Strictly Business
Out of Love

Twin Find Series:
Strictly Family
Out of Office

Bachelor Tower Series:
Insatiable Bachelor
Impossible Bachelor
Undeniable Bachelor

Lone Star Burn Series:
Taken, Not Spurred
Tycoon Takedown
Taken Home
Taking Charge

A Lighthearted Utensil Romance
Forked
Spooned
Knifed

Temptation Series:
Untouchable Kate

About the Author

Ruth Cardello was born the youngest of 11 children in a small city in southern Massachusetts. She spent her young adult years moving as far away as she could from her large extended family. She lived in Boston, Paris, Orlando, New York—then came full circle and moved back to New England. She now happily lives one town over from the one she was born in. For her, family trumped the warmer weather and international scene.

She was an educator for 20 years, the last 11 as a kindergarten teacher. When her school district began cutting jobs, Ruth turned a serious eye toward her second love—writing and has never been happier. When she's not writing, you can find her chasing her children around her small farm, riding her horses, or connecting with her readers online.

Contact Ruth:

Website: RuthCardello.com
Email: RCardello@RuthCardello.com
FaceBook: Author Ruth Cardello
TikTok: tiktok.com/@author.ruthcardello

Made in the USA
Columbia, SC
31 March 2025